IS THERE ANY OTHER SERVICE I CAN PERFORM FOR YOU?

"Yes", Crane said, staring at the computer's screen. "You can come up with the identity of the murderer."

THERE ARE NUMEROUS HYPOTHESES. THE MURDERER IS A PSYCHOTIC. THE MURDERER CRAVES EXPOSURE. THE MURDERER . . .

"Stop," ordered Crane. "You simply don't understand human psychology."

YOU ARE IN ERROR. I CAN ANALYZE YOU. YOU ARE A COMPULSIVE OVER-ACHIEVER AND YOU ARE SEXUALLY ATTRACTED TO THE BLACK PEARL.

"You're crazy," snapped Crane. "The murderer is not! I'm telling you—the body was deliberately moved. And the only sane reason is that the killer is trying to force someone else's hand!"

THEN HIS NEXT MOVE IS TO KILL AGAIN. . . .

TALES OF THE VELVET COMET #2

EROS AT ZENITH

MIKE RESNICK

A SIGNET BOOK

NEW AMERICAN LIBRARY

NAL BOOKS ARE AVAILABLE AT QUANTITY DISCOUNTS WHEN USED TO PROMOTE PRODUCTS OR SERVICES. FOR INFORMATION PLEASE WRITE TO PREMIUM MARKETING DIVISION, NEW AMERICAN LIBRARY, 1633 BROADWAY, NEW YORK, NEW YORK 10019.

Cover art by Kevin E. Johnson

A hardcover edition of *Eros at Zenith* was published by Phantasia Press.

SIGNET TRADEMARK REG. U.S. PAT. OFF. AND FOREIGN COUNTRIES
REGISTERED TRADEMARK—MARCA REGISTRADA
HECHO EN CHICAGO, U.S.A.

SIGNET, SIGNET CLASSIC, MENTOR, PLUME, MERIDIAN AND NAL BOOKS are published by New American Library, 1633 Broadway, New York, New York 10019

First Signet Printing, July, 1985

1 2 3 4 5 6 7 8 9

PRINTED IN THE UNITED STATES OF AMERICA

To Carol, as always,

And to Sid Altus: publisher, editor, and friend—who is occasionally permitted to win at poker so that he'll keep buying my books.

PROLOGUE

The *Velvet Comet* spun slowly in space, resembling nothing more than a giant barbell. Its metal skin glistened a brilliant silver, and its array of flashing lights could be seen from literally tens of thousands of miles away.

Seventeen different engineering firms had worked on its design, thousands of men and machines had spent millions of hours on its construction, and it housed a permanent staff of more than six hundred men and women. Owned and financed by the Vainmill Syndicate, the largest of the Republic's conglomerates, it had been built in orbit around the distant planet of Charlemagne, but now it circled Deluros VIII, the huge world that would someday become the capital planet of the race of Man.

During its forty-six years of existence it had become a byword for opulence and elegance, a synonym for hedonism and dissipation. Its fame had spread to the most remote worlds of the Republic, and while its Sybaritic luxuries and even its air of exclusivity were often imitated, they were never equalled.

The *Velvet Comet*, after more than three decades of gestation, had been born in space, and less than a century after its birth it would die in space, mourned by few and forgotten by most. But in the meantime, it did its living with a grace and style that would not be seen again for many millenia.

It was the crown jewel in the Syndicate's Entertainment and Leisure Division, a showplace where the rich and the famous—and occasionally the notorious—gathered to see and be seen, to conspicuously consume, and to revel in pleasures which were designed to satisfy even the most jaded of tastes. For while the *Velvet Comet* housed a compendium of the finest shops and boutiques, of gourmet restaurants and elegant lounges, while it boasted a fabulous casino and a score of other entertainments, it was first and foremost a brothel.

And it was the brothel, and the promises of secret delights that it proffered, that enticed its select clientele out to the *Comet*. They came from Deluros VIII and a thousand nearby and distant worlds. Money was no object to these men and women; they came to play, and to relax, and to indulge.

And one of them came to kill.

1.

"Name?"

Crane stared impatiently at the security woman.

"You know perfectly well who I am."

"I'm sorry, sir," she persisted. "But I can't pass you through the airlock unless you tell me your name."

Crane looked briefly at the other people lined up behind him, shrugged, and turned back to the security woman. "Andrew Jackson Crane," he said at last.

"Point of origin?"

"Deluros VIII."

"Thank you, Mr. Crane," she said, looking down at her computer. "Your voiceprint has been cleared and you are free to enter the *Comet*."

"Fine. What do I do now?"

"Step through into the Mall. I have been informed that someone will be waiting for you."

Crane grunted an acknowledgement and walked out into the Mall, the opulent two-mile long row of shops and boutiques that formed the bar between the two bells of the *Velvet Comet*. There was a strip of parquet flooring some sixty feet wide running down the entire length of it, which in turn was flanked by two slidewalks that slowly moved past the shops.

"Mr. Crane?"

Crane turned and found himself facing a short, rather stocky man dressed in the green uniform of the *Comet's* security crew.

"Yes?"

"My name is Paxton Oglevie," said the man. "My instructions are to take you to see the body."

Crane frowned. "And who gave you those instructions?"

"The Chief of Security, sir."

"Why isn't he here to greet me himself?" demanded Crane.

"*Her*self," corrected Oglevie. "I really couldn't say, sir."

"Well, *I* could. She may not like the fact that I've been put in charge of this case, but that's no excuse for her not to be here." He paused. "Where's the body now?"

"In the hospital."

"Where's that?"

"About half a mile to your left, sir."

Crane looked down the Mall in the direction indicated. "Don't you have an infirmary in the crew's quarters?"

"Yes, sir," said Oglevie.

"Then why carry it through the Mall when we're trying to hush this thing up?"

"Because the infirmary doesn't have the facilities

to store dead bodies, sir," replied Oglevie. "I assure you we were very discreet."

"I'll just bet," muttered Crane. He turned back to Oglevie. "Have they performed an autopsy yet?"

"We were awaiting your instructions, sir."

"First thing you've done right so far," said Crane. "Well, it's waited this long; I suppose it can wait another hour. Take me to the Black Pearl."

"The Black Pearl, sir?" repeated Oglevie.

"She's in charge of this place, isn't she?"

"Yes. But my orders were to—"

"I'm giving you new orders," said Crane firmly.

"She's quite busy, sir," protested Oglevie.

"She'll see *me*."

"But—"

"I haven't got all day," said Crane, heading off toward a slidewalk. "If you won't take me to her, I'll have to find her myself."

"Just a moment, sir," said Oglevie in resignation.

Crane stopped and turned to him.

"That slidewalk goes to the Home," explained the security man.

"The Home?" repeated Crane.

"The crews' quarters. You want the Resort," he said, heading across the parquet flooring toward the other slidewalk. "If you'll follow me, sir."

Crane fell into step behind him, and a moment later was gliding silently past the exclusive shops that catered to the refined and cultivated tastes of the *Comet's* clientele. There were softly-lit jewelry stores specializing in gems totally unknown to human worlds, tasteful art galleries offering the finest work of a dozen different races, stylish dress designers whose offerings ranged from the bizarre to the unique, haberdashers who would create a complete wardrobe before the patron's stay aboard the *Comet* was over, exquisite antique shops (one of which actually displayed a shelf of leather-bound books from Earth itself), a dozen exclusive lingerie shops dealing in the erotic and the merely exotic, half a dozen branches of well-known brokerage houses, a tobacco shop that stocked the finest cigars of a hundred worlds, an incredibly expensive florist that imported fresh flowers daily from Deluros VIII, and literally hundreds of other shops and boutiques.

Crane watched the shops glide by until his initial fascination wore off, then began scrutinizing the shoppers, trying, for his own amusement, to separate the prostitutes of both sexes from the patrons. Sometimes, especially when the patron was showing signs of age, it was a simple matter; but frequently, to his surprise, it was not. Most of the people he observed were dressed tastefully, and even those wearing revealing apparel seemed more elegant than blatant. Most of them seemed happy and content, and he concluded that this was perhaps the one place they could relax without the continual fear of robbery, kidnapping, or worse.

Which brought him back to business.

"Have you turned up any fingerprints?" he asked Oglevie.

"Not yet, sir. It looks like a careful, professional job."

"Any trace of the murder weapon?"

"None."

"I thought your security system was supposed to be tamperproof," said Crane. "Has anyone figured out yet how the killer got around it?"

"No, sir."

Crane frowned. "Has anyone done *anything* yet?"

"I assume so," replied Oglevie noncommittally. "I was in the Resort when it was discovered," he added. "When I reported back this morning, I was told to meet you at the airlock."

"What's your Security Chief's name?" demanded Crane.

"The Dragon Lady."

Crane snorted. "Dragon Lady. Black Pearl. Doesn't anyone use a real name around this place?"

"Very infrequently, sir," answered Oglevie. "It tends to spoil the illusion."

"What's *your* real name?"

"Paxton Oglevie," replied the security man. "But of course, I rarely deal with the patrons."

"Well, Paxton Oglevie, once I get to the Black Pearl's office, wherever that may be, I suggest that you hunt up your Dragon Lady and tell her I want to see her as soon as I've examined the body."

"And how soon will that be, sir?" asked Oglevie, nodding politely to an extremely handsome young man who waved to him from the opposing slidewalk on the far side of the strip of parquet flooring.

"I haven't the slightest idea," said Crane. "Maybe an hour, maybe two."

"Wouldn't it be easier to summon her when you're ready, rather than—?"

"First of all, Oglevie, that wasn't a request," said Crane. "Second, a murder has been committed here, and the Chief of Security had better *not* have anything better to do with her time than help me solve it." He paused. "And third, I tend to become very unpleasant when my authority is questioned."

Oglevie shrugged and said nothing.

They rode the slidewalk another half-mile in silence. Then Crane turned to the security man again.

"What's that vibration beneath us?"

"The tramway, sir."

"That's where you found the body?"

"Yes, sir."

"It runs the whole length of the shopping mall?" asked Crane. Oglevie nodded. "And also stops at the airlock?"

"Yes, sir."

"Are there any other entrances or exits to it?"

"None, sir. The tramcar stops only at each end and at the airlock."

"And of course only the *Comet's* personnel are permitted to ride it, so that the customers will have to pass by all the stores on the way in and again on the way out, right?"

"Yes, sir—and we call them *patrons*."

"Call them anything you want," said Crane. "I'm not one of them, and the next time I direct you to take me somewhere you can skip the scenic route."

Oglevie made no reply, and in another three minutes they reached the end of the Mall.

"Follow me, sir," said the security man, stepping onto the parquet flooring and heading off toward an ornate reception foyer.

"What level are we on?" asked Crane.

"The main one, sir," replied Oglevie. "There are three levels beneath us, composed entirely of suites for our patrons."

"And above us?"

"Various recreational areas."

"The fantasy rooms that I've heard so much about?" asked Crane.

"Yes, sir. And now, if you'll just wait here for a moment, I'll inform the Black Pearl that you've arrived."

Crane watched the stocky security man walk to a bank of computers that had been set into one of the foyer's walls, then examined his new surroundings. The foyer was an octagonal room, perhaps eighty feet across, with numerous plush couches and contour chairs, about half of which were occupied by couples and small groups. Clustered in one corner were a number of men and women who were watching stock market quotations and sporting results flash across a pair of large screens. Three elegantly-tailored cocktail waiters circulated through the foyer dispensing free drinks, while four young women worked a registration desk. Crane looked up and saw that the domed ceiling had an enormous pornographic tableau done in bas-relief.

Finally he looked back down the Mall, which from this perspective looked like a polished chrome-and-glass corridor extending to infinity. He noticed that a magician had set up shop about eighty yards from the entrance to the foyer, and was amusing passers-by with his sleight-of-hand tricks. Then an elderly woman, weighted down with a massive diamond necklace and a totally unnecessary wrap made from the fur of some bluetinted alien animal, walked out of a nearby boutique and began approaching the foyer. Crane studied her, put her age at somewhere between seventy and eighty, and spent a few moments appraising her jewelry. He had valued her multitude of rings and bracelets at somewhere between four and five million credits, and was just about to go to work on the necklace when he felt a hand on his shoulder.

"She'll see you now," said Oglevie.

"Then let's go."

Oglevie headed off to his left, Crane followed him, and a moment later they began passing a number of restaurants, each unique in its decor. One resembled a sanitized and opulent version of one of the notorious drug dens of Altair III, another was a formal, candle-lit affair featuring crisp linen tablecloths, fine china and silver, and servants in powdered wigs and Revolutionary America costumes, while a third was simply a huge silk tent in which the customers sat or reclined on large cushions and ate off a long, very low table.

"How late are these places open?" asked Crane, suddenly realizing that he hadn't eaten in quite some time.

"Around the clock, sir," replied Oglevie. "There is no day or night aboard the *Velvet Comet*."

"I thought I was told that the body was discovered at 0200 hours, ship's time," said Crane sharply.

"Two in the morning," nodded Oglevie. "That would be about right, sir. When I said that we had no day or night, I meant of course that we are a 24-hour-a-day operation."

"Of course," repeated Crane.

They passed a cocktail lounge filled with angular chrome chairs and polished obsidian tables.

"What the hell is *that?*" demanded Crane suddenly.

"What, sir?"

"That man with the make-up job," said Crane, indicating a middle-aged man with bright red lips and black grease paint which had been applied in a diamond-shaped pattern that made it appear as if he were crying. "He sure as hell can't be a customer."

"No, sir. He works here."

"Are you trying to tell me women find that attractive?" asked Crane. "Because if you are . . ."

"I really couldn't say, sir. His name's Pagliacci. He works as a comedian in one of the nightclubs."

"I hope his jokes are funnier than his make-up."

"I've never caught his act, sir," replied Oglevie.

Crane took a final look at the comedian, shook his head, and once again fell into step behind Oglevie. After another few minutes they came to a large, ornate door.

"This is the place?" asked Crane.

Oglevie nodded. "I'll wait outside for you, sir."

"That won't be necessary. I don't know how long I'll be, so you might as well go back to work."

Oglevie looked relieved. "As you wish, sir."

Crane watched the security man walk away, then turned to the door. He was just about to reach out and press a small buzzer when it slid back into the wall, revealing a spacious and tastefully-furnished office. The beige carpeting was deep and luxuriant, there was a well-stocked hardwood bar on the back wall, and a pair of fur-covered couches faced each other across a large chrome coffee table which he suspected was also a computer. Half a dozen computer screens were set unobtrusively into one wall, while holographs and paintings were carefully hung on the remaining walls. A pair of stylish chrome chairs faced an artificial fireplace that was made of highly-polished opalescent quartz which seemed to catch the indirect lighting of the room and reflect it back in a myriad of changing colors.

As the door slid shut behind him, Crane stepped into the office and began scrutinizing it more carefully. The holographs on the wall instantly captured his attention, and he walked over and stood before them. There were eleven, each displaying the likeness of a lovely and exotically-clad woman, and he paused to examine them individually.

"My predecessors," said a feminine voice.

He turned and saw a tall, slender, strikingly beautiful black woman standing in a doorway just to the right of the fireplace.

Her hair was piled high atop her head, strung through with shining gold beads. He single garment was a glittering strip of metallic gold cloth, carefully wound around her body in a series of spirals that exposed almost as much as it concealed. Large circular golden earrings, a number of golden bracelets, and a pair of delicate golden sandals completed the picture.

"You're the Black Pearl?" he said.

"Good old lucky Number Thirteen," she replied with a grimace. "You must be Mr. Crane here to bring the murderer to justice."

"There are only eleven holographs on the wall," he noted.

"The Corporation decorated my office, and for some reason saw fit not to display one of the holographs." She smiled. "I assure you that there really have been twelve previous madams."

"I've never met a madam before," he said awkwardly. "How does one address you?"

"As the Black Pearl," she replied. "It's my name." She paused, obviously amused by his uneasiness. "I, on the other hand, have never met a detective before."

"For all I know, neither has your Chief of Security," said Crane. "At least, she hasn't met *this* one."

"She's probably busy trying to solve the crime before you take over," remarked the Black Pearl. "She's a very proud woman, the Dragon Lady."

"She's also a very frightened one," added Crane. "And not without cause."

"Why should you say that, Mr. Crane?"

"Because a patron was killed in an area that patrons theoretically can't gain access to. That means your security system has been breached, and she's in charge of it."

"Then shouldn't you be talking to her instead of me?"

"I plan to," he said ominously. "In the meantime, I thought I ought to meet the person in charge of the ship."

"Well, now that you're here," she said, walking to the bar, "can I fix you a drink?"

He shook his head. "I don't drink."

She sighed. "I suppose you disapprove of prostitution and gambling, too."

"I haven't given it any thought."

"That's just as bad," she said with a chuckle. "If enough people don't think about it, we're out of business."

He stared at her for a long moment. "You don't seem very upset about what's happened up here."

"Of course I am," replied the Black Pearl. "But I've got 509 very wealthy, very demanding prima donnas on board who'll be even more upset if I stop tending to their comforts." She stared at him. "Or have I got 510?"

"I'm not sure I understand you," said Crane.

"If your understanding is that faulty, you're never going to catch our killer, Mr. Crane," said the Black Pearl. "You're here to complain because the Dragon Lady wasn't at the airlock to meet you."

"Am I?"

She nodded. "It's the only subject that seems to interest you so far."

"There are others," he said. "For one thing, I'll need a place to stay until this case is over."

"In the Home?"

"I'd prefer one of the suites in the Resort," said Crane.

"They're very expensive."

"Vainmill will pay for it. And arrange to have all my meals billed to Vainmill."

"You certainly like your comfort."

"Yes, I do. Have you any objection?"

"Not at all," she replied. "I approve whole-heartedly of people who like their comfort. Will you be wanting a companion for your suite?"

"I hadn't given it any thought," he responded.

"Ah, that's right: you don't think about such things. Well, if you get lonely, let us know." She walked over to a couch. "Do you mind if I sit down, Mr. Crane?"

"Suit yourself," he said with a shrug, looking away as she lowered herself to the couch and readjusted her outfit.

"Don't be embarrassed," she said. "These are just my working clothes. I can get a robe if my outfit distracts you."

"How you people choose to dress is a matter of complete indifference to me," said Crane.

"How disappointing," she replied with mock regret.

"Now," he said, seating himself opposite her and returning to his subject with a single-minded intensity, "about your Security Chief."

"All right, Mr. Crane," sighed the Black Pearl. "What *about* my Security Chief?"

"Her failure to meet me was more than a breach of etiquette. It shows a blatant disregard for my authority, and I want to determine wheher or not it represents an unwillingness on her part to accept Vainmill's decision to send me here."

"Mr. Crane, I appreciate your concern, but there *is* a murderer walking the decks of the *Comet*. Wouldn't you be better advised to go searching for him instead of sitting here arguing about protocol?"

"I'll catch him, never fear," said Crane. "I just want to make sure we understand each other before I begin my investigation."

"I think we understand each other very well," she responded easily. "You're concerned with social graces and I'm concerned with apprehending a killer. Given our respective professions, doesn't that seem a little backward to you?"

"Do you plan to answer my question or not?" he demanded.

"You haven't asked one. Look," she said reasonably, "I'm not the enemy, Mr. Crane. Neither is the Dragon Lady. We are both fully prepared to give you whatever assistance you require. The enemy is out there"—she nodded her head toward the door—"quite possibly preparing to kill again."

Crane stared at her for a moment. "I realize that people find me abrasive and demanding . . ." he began.

"You left out tyrannical," she noted dryly.

"And tyrannical," he acknowledged. "I can't do anything about the abrasiveness, and I freely admit to being demanding. I'm dedicated to my work, and I expect my subordinates to be just as dedicated. I will not tolerate laziness, disobedience, or insubordination. As long as everyone keeps that in mind, I can be a reasonably pleasant person to get along with."

"Then we both have the same goal," she answered. "You won't tolerate sloppy work in hunting down the murderer, and I won't tolerate a continued threat to my patrons. I see no reason why we can't work together." She paused. "I just hope you're as good a detective as Vainmill seems to think you are."

"Better," he said unselfconsciously. "And I'm more than a detective—I'm a damage control expert."

"Do we need one?"

"If the patrons find out what's happened, you're going to need a dozen of them," he replied. "How many people know about it so far?"

"Not counting the doctors who might have examined the body, there are just four of us," said the Black Pearl. "The maintenance man who found the body, the Dragon Lady, the security woman who helped her move it, and myself."

"Five," he corrected her. "You're forgetting Oglevie."

"That's right," she said, nodding her head. "And he's so eminently forgettable, too. How *is* Uriah Heep this morning?"

He frowned. "Uriah . . .?"

She smiled. "Don't worry about it. It's just my pet name for him. I suppose the Dragon Lady had to tell him so that he wouldn't be so surprised that he repeated it at the top of his lungs when you mentioned it to him."

"I take it you don't think too much of Mr. Oglevie?" noted Crane.

"As a matter of fact, I try not to think of him at all," she replied. "Still, he's the Dragon Lady's second in command."

"Really? I wouldn't have guessed it from his manner."

"There are no end of things you wouldn't guess from his manner," she said. She shot him a quick glance. "I see the wheels starting to turn, Mr. Crane. Forget it. Paxton Oglevie wouldn't have the intestinal fortitude to kill one of the insects he so closely resembles."

"Then why have you gone out of your way to give me an unflattering picture of him?" he asked her.

"Because you're probably going to have to spend some time in his company, and I felt you should be forewarned. After all, that's what friends are for—and you and I are going to be friends, Mr. Crane."

"Are we?"

She nodded firmly. "Absolutely—unless you can think of some reason why we should be enemies."

"None."

"Then it's settled." She looked across at him, studying his face. "You know," she remarked after a moment, "you might be an attractive man if you would just smile occasionally."

"I'm not in a funny business," he said.

"Neither am I, when you get right down to it," she replied. "Yet I smile all the time."

"I'll smile when I catch the murderer."

"Just how difficult do you expect that to be?" she asked seriously.

"Well," he said, "we've got a closed environment here, and a reasonably thorough security system. I'll check out the body and the area where the murder occurred, begin comparing alibis against the record, have the computer put together a history of the victim, and with a little hard work and a little luck I ought to be able to clear this thing up before too long."

He was right about the methodology, but wrong about the result.

2.

Crane found his way back to the foyer with no difficulty, then took the escalator down to the tramway entrance. A small titanium gate barred his way, and he waited for the computer to check his retinagram.

"I'm sorry, sir," said a voice. "But the tramway is for use by *Comet* personnel only."

"Who is this?" demanded Crane.

"Security guard Enoch Lyman, sir," was the response.

"I assume you're not in my immediate vicinity?"

"That is correct."

"My name is Andrew Jackson Crane, I work for the Váinmill Syndicate, and I'm here on official business. You can check me out with either Paxton Oglevie or the Black Pearl."

"One moment, please." There was a brief period of silence. "Mr. Oglevie has confirmed your identity, Mr. Crane. If you will step up to the computer once again, I will program it to recognize and respond to your retinagram."

Crane did as he was told, standing in front of the computer's scanning lens.

"All right, sir," said Lyman's voice. "You will have access to the tramway and the Home for the duration of your stay here."

The gate slid back, and Crane stepped through to a small platform, where he boarded the enclosed tramcar. He commanded it to start, felt a slight pressure due to the rapid acceleration, and got off when it stopped at the airlock some 80 seconds later.

He took an escalator to the main level, found that it bypassed the airlock and let him off inside the Mall, and was shortly riding a slidewalk to the hospital.

There was a rather small woman waiting for him outside the hospital door. She wore an austerely-tailored burgundy gown, sleeveless and high-collared, on which a dragon had been embroidered in metallic gold thread. It spiralled around her body, and the head seemed to insinuate its way over her left shoulder and come to rest across her breasts, glaring at the world with jeweled eyes.

The woman herself had very short black hair that was touched with gray. She had managed to accumulate a few excess pounds over the years, but Crane could tell at a glance that she had once been quite beautiful. There was a hint of the Oriental about her face, though each of her features seemed Caucasian. Except for a small platinum-and-ruby ring she wore no jewelry of any kind, and kept her make-up to a minimum.

"You're the Dragon Lady?" Crane asked.

"And you must be Mr. Crane."

"Where the hell have you been?" he demanded.

"Now, *that's* a cordial greeting," she replied dryly.

"It's better than the one you gave me," said Crane. "Where were you?"

"Busy."

"Doing what?"

"Tightening the security in the Resort. We can *assume* that none of the patrons are in any danger, but we can't *know* it."

He considered her answer for a moment.

"All right," he said at last. "I approve."

"Thank you," she replied with a hint of irony.

"I thought all Security personnel wore green uniforms," he noted.

"All except me."

"Any particular reason?"

"It's part of the illusion," she explained.

"I don't follow you."

"When you came through the airlock, Mr. Crane, you stepped into a fantasy world. Aboard the *Velvet Comet* the mask is more important than the face. I am the Dragon Lady; therefore I dress like the Dragon Lady. This is my public persona."

"And no one else in Security has a mask?" he inquired wryly.

"*Their* mask is a green uniform," she replied with a smile. "Mine isn't. It's one of the nice things about being Chief of Security." She gestured toward the door. "Shall we go inside?"

He nodded and followed her into the hospital. It was a small but efficient complex, with private facilities for treating up to 30 patients, two operating theaters, a pair of physical therapy rooms, a low-gravity ward for heart patients, and a number of diagnostic centers. The walls gleamed a cheerful yellow, the floor was tan and polished, the atmosphere seemed expensive and formal. The overall impression Crane got was one of luxurious efficiency. He couldn't imagine that the standard cuisine here differed markedly from that of the Resort, or that the prostitutes weren't encouraged to stop by the sickbay now and then to give a patient some special therapy.

"The hospital doesn't have a mortuary, so we put him in here," said the Dragon Lady, stopping by a door bearing an OBSERVATION WARD notation.

"Nobody saw you bring him in?"

She shook her head. "There were only two patients here at the time. One was sound asleep, and the other was in surgery."

"How about the patrons in the Mall?" asked Crane.

"There's a service area below the tramway level. We brought him here on a truck lift, and took him in through the service entrance."

"Well, at least somebody did *something* right," he commented.

"How thoughtful of you to notice," she replied.

She recited a six-digit code, and a moment later the door slid back. The ward contained four beds, each capable of being tied into a bank of life support systems. Three of the beds were empty; the fourth contained a nude male body.

Crane sniffed the air and made a face: even the filtration system couldn't totally mask the odor.

"How long has he been dead?" he asked.

"The one doctor who's been allowed to see him estimates that he died between 64 and 72 hours before we brought him here. We'll have a more accurate idea after the autopsy."

"And his name is Edward Infante?"

"That's right."

"Have you run a computer check on him?"

"Of course. All the information is back at my office, though I can call it up on one of the hospital's computers if you'd like to see it."

"Later," answered Crane. "Unless there's something in it that might tell us who would want to kill him."

"Not at first reading."

Crane had been walking around the bed, looking at the body. Finally he stopped and placed his hands on his hips.

"Where the hell is the wound?"

"Just behind the ear," she replied.

He rolled the body onto its side. "Not big enough for a knife," he commented, staring at the single puncture mark. "It looks like something about the size of an old-fashioned knitting needle. How deep is it?"

"About eleven centimeters, according to the doctor."

"That'd do it," he muttered. "Nice and neat. And dangerous."

"Dangerous?" repeated the Dragon Lady sardonically. "It was deadly."

"Dangerous to the killer," replied Crane, examining the wound. "Do it right and you kill instantly; do it wrong and you've got a flesh wound or else you break off the point of your weapon against the skull, and your victim starts screaming bloody murder." He looked up. "Well, that narrows down our list of suspects."

"To someone who would be skilled enough to hit the right spot on the first try?" suggested the Dragon Lady.

He shook his head. "You'll never pull that kind of information out of your personnel files."

"Then I don't follow you."

"There are surer ways to kill a man," he said. "Why do you suppose our killer chose this method?"

"Guns and laser weapons can be traced."

"Of course," he said impatiently. "But why not slit his throat or stab him in the heart? Even if you botch it, he's still going to die in a couple of minutes."

"He'd have time to scream for help," said the Dragon Lady.

Crane looked irritated. "You're not thinking. I already told you: he'd have time to scream for help no matter how you screwed it up."

"If you know something I don't know, Mr. Crane," she said, "why don't you just tell me what it is? I've been up for almost 24 hours, and I'm in no mood for guessing games."

Crane stared at her coldly for a moment, then shrugged. "This wasn't a lucky blow," he said at last. "The killer knew exactly what he was doing. To the untrained eye, everything back there looks like bone; if you don't know anatomy, you're a hundred times more likely to stab someone from the front, where everything looks soft—or if you *have* to stab from behind, you go for the middle of the back and hope to hit a vital organ. And since our killer knew what he was doing, he also knew he was taking a chance. A quarter of an inch up or down and he's blown it. So why would he go for the most difficult kill?"

"You're asking questions again."

"Because there's no blood," he explained. "You stab a man from in front and you're more likely to kill him, but you're going to get spattered with his blood in the process. This way is clean."

"So you think the killer couldn't afford to get blood on himself?"

"I *know* it," answered Crane. "So that narrows down our list of suspects to people who had to appear in public right after the murder, people who didn't have a chance to change their clothing."

"You're wrong," said the Dragon Lady firmly.

"The hell I am."

"*Everyone* appears in public when they get off the tram," she pointed out. "After all, it only goes to the Resort, the Mall, and the Home. There are people and security cameras in all three locations."

Crane shook his head impatiently. "The killer was carrying his weapon, and he had figured out how to beat the tramway's security system, which means that this was a premeditated murder—and *that* means he could easily have hidden some clothing in the tunnel if he'd wanted to. It took you a couple of days to find the body; there was no reason to assume that you'd find a fresh change of clothes any sooner. No, he had to kill him in this manner because he only had a couple of minutes, tops, before he was due to appear elsewhere."

"That still doesn't help much," remarked the Dragon Lady. "During the eight-hour period when the murder occurred, the computer says that more than 200 people took the tram; I already checked it out. You'd have to pinpoint the time almost to the minute before your conclusion will be of any use to us."

"I will," he said emphatically.

"How? Even the autopsy can't help that much."

He shrugged. "I don't know yet; I just got here."

"And yet you're certain you can do it?"

"Absolutely."

"You're a very confident young man, Mr. Crane," she remarked.

"Not without cause," he replied.

"So I've been told."

"Oh?"

She nodded. "When I was informed that you would be in charge of the case, I spent some time checking up on you."

"And what did you find out?"

"Andrew Jackson Crane," she recited. "Age, 28. Height, six feet two inches. Weight, 161 pounds. Unmarried. Graduated with honors at 20, master's degree at 21. Joined Vainmill's Security Division on Komornos in the Atria system, transferred to Spica II within the year, transferred to Deluros VIII two years later. Nine promotions in seven years, currently the Syndicate's chief detective and troubleshooter in the Deluros and Canphor systems. Specialty: murder. 28 assignments, all completed successfully."

"Is there anything else?"

"Only that you have expressed dissatisfaction at not yet obtaining a supervisory position, and that your associates find you difficult and demanding to work with."

"That's because I *am* difficult and demanding to work with," he said, not without a trace of pride. "As for my associates, they're a bunch of maladroits and incompetents."

"I hope you will find me an improvement," said the Dragon Lady.

"I'll let you know." Crane took a final look at the

corpse. "I've seen all there is to see here," he announced. "Tell the doctor to save some tissue samples from the wound and ship the body to whoever wants to bury it, once he's through with the autopsy."

The Dragon Lady entered the order on a small computer by the bed.

"All right," said Crane. "I want to get something to eat, and then we'll take a look at where you found him."

"There's a small commissary in the Home, very near Security headquarters," she suggested.

"I'm sure there is," said Crane. "But I'll eat at the Resort."

"Shall I meet you when you're through?"

"You're coming with me."

"I have a lot of work to do," said the Dragon Lady.

"None of it is more important than catching a murderer."

"Also, I'm really not very hungry."

"Then you can watch me eat."

He walked out into the corridor, and after locking the room she turned and followed him.

"How many doctors does the hospital have?" he asked, looking into an empty therapy room.

"Three," she replied.

"Eight-hour shifts?"

"Unless there's an emergency."

"I imagine most of their work consists of surreptitiously treating various social diseases."

"Why should you think so?" she asked.

"Because I saw a scanner in the airlock. I suspect that no one gets past the security team until they check out clean, and that if they don't pass muster, they're discreetly directed to the hospital."

"You don't miss much, I'll grant you that," commented the Dragon Lady.

They exited the hospital and stepped out into the Mall, which was a little busier now than when he had first arrived, then took the slidewalk to the airlock and descended to the tramway level.

"Where did you find the body?" he asked as they reached the small platform.

"About 250 yards from the Resort," she replied. "You can't see it from here."

"How often does the tram run?"

"That depends," said the Dragon Lady. "It can get from the Resort to the Home in about two minutes nonstop, three if it stops at the airlock. But once it's empty it will stay where it is until the computer notifies it that someone is waiting on a different platform. During our peak periods it's in constant motion, but there are times when it's not in use for ten or twelve minutes at a stretch."

The tram arrived, and they entered the car, which also contained two handsome young men and a satin-and-feather-clad woman who were on their way from the Home to the Resort. They rode in silence for 80 seconds, then emerged from the car, ascended to the foyer, and were soon walking toward the *Comet's* complement of gourmet restaurants.

"Which one's the best?" asked Crane.

"They're all very good," replied the Dragon Lady.

"Fine. Recommend one."

She scrutinized him carefully. "I think you might like the Cosmic Room," she suggested.

"Lead the way."

She walked past three restaurants, then paused before an ornate door.

"You don't suffer from vertigo, do you?" she asked him.

"No."

"Good."

She opened the door, and they stepped through it onto a narrow transparent walkway. Crane's first impression was that he had suddenly intruded upon the birth of the Universe. The room seemed to extend to infinity, and all about him were exploding stars and embryonic galaxies whirling through space. Here was a meteor swarm, there a spinning star cluster, off to his left a quasar shooting its matter billions of miles into the void. Suddenly he became aware of the fact that he, too, was in motion, and he reached for a narrow railing to steady himself.

"It's all done with holographic projections," she said matter-of-factly, "but it *does* make an impressive display, doesn't it?"

"Very," he answered. "Is the room moving?"

"It rotates very slowly."

He studied his surroundings again, and this time he was able to pick out about a dozen tables located randomly throughout the room, each at a different height. Then a comet shot off into space, and two more tables were revealed.

"How big is this place?"

"The room or the capacity?" she asked.

"Both."

"Well, the room is about 60 by 80 feet, and perhaps 20 feet high. It holds 24 tables, though the projectors are programmed so that you can never see more than 14 at once. This walkway we're on eventually leads to each of them."

Suddenly the *maitre d'* approached them and

warmly greeted the Dragon Lady. Then, as an afterthought, he turned to Crane.

"Have you a reservation, sir?" he asked.

"No," said Crane.

"Then I'm afraid that—"

"Give us the house table," interrupted the Dragon Lady.

"Excuse me," he said placatingly. "I didn't realize you were together. You are so rarely accompanied by—"

"The table," repeated the Dragon Lady.

The *maitre d'* bowed and immediately led them up a steep incline where they could look down at the death throes of a galaxy as it was drawn into a black hole of ever-increasing dimensions.

Crane spent another few minutes observing the room, then looked at his menu.

"You're sure you're not hungry?" he said.

"Positive."

He shrugged. "Suit yourself. But I want you to have some coffee; you won't be any use to me if you're sleepy."

He signalled to a waiter, ordered soup, a mutated shellfish in cream sauce, and two cups of coffee.

"All right," he said to her after the waiter had left. "We might as well get to know each other, as long as we're going to be working together—which means that *I* might as well get to know *you*, since you've already read my dossier." He paused. "How long have you been Chief of Security here?"

"19 years."

"And before that?"

"I was a security guard here for six years."

"25 years is a long time to spend in one place," he commented.

"29 years, Mr. Crane."

"Not unless my addition is wrong."

"I was a prostitute for four years," said the Dragon Lady.

"Oh?"

She nodded.

"A prostitute on this ship makes a lot more than a security guard," he said. "What made you change?"

"I could see the handwriting on the wall, and I liked the ambience of the *Comet*."

"What handwriting?"

"Look around you, Mr. Crane," she replied. "The men and women who work here are the finest physical specimens you're going to find anywhere in the Republic. And after four years of starving myself and working out in the gym every day, I figured it was a losing battle." She smiled. "You can't imagine how I dreaded those Thursday weigh-ins."

"You make it sound like you're all athletes," he said.

"We are," replied the Dragon Lady. "With one exception—*our* season never ends. Anyway, I looked around to see what else I could do, and since I'm neither a chef nor a technician, I applied for a job in Security, and they accepted me."

"How long does the average prostitute last here?" asked Crane curiously.

"The *Comet* has no *average* prostitutes."

"You know what I mean," he said with a touch of irritation.

"Three to five years," she replied. "I think eight is the record, even for our madams. No, I take that back: we had one, before my time, called the Leather Madonna, who made it for ten years."

"I wish I knew where you people get your names," said Crane.

"I never knew her, so I have no idea how she came by hers," said the Dragon Lady. She paused as the waiter delivered their coffee and Crane's soup. "Anyway, Security is a different story. Do you know that I'm only the second Chief of Security in the *Comet's* 46 years of existence?"

"No, I didn't know," said Crane, sipping his soup.

"It's true. My predecessor, a man named Rasputin," —Crane winced, but said nothing—"took me under his wing, so to speak, and taught me everything I know. And I've been a damned good Security Chief, too. I was rather hoping to retire with an unblemished record," she added regretfully.

"You're off the hook on this one," he replied. "If we don't come up with the killer, it's my neck that'll be on the chopping block, not yours."

She shook her head. "It happened while *I* was in charge of the ship's security."

"Then we'll catch him while you're in charge of the ship's security, and everyone will be happy," said Crane, finishing his soup. "That was excellent," he said, indicating the empty bowl. "If the rest of the meal is like this, I'm surprised that *all* the employees aren't lugging around a little extra weight."

"No one can eat meals like this every day," she said. "Not even me. They're much too rich."

"*I* can."

"But you're a very tense, very energetic young man. You work it all off." She appraised him thoughtfully. "Actually, you could do with fifteen more pounds."

"Is that your professional opinion?" he asked sardonically.

"Of course not," she said with a laugh. "Professionally, all a patron ever had to be was alive, healthy, and possessed of a proper credit rating."

"And a man," added Crane.

"Usually."

He was about to say something when the waiter reappeared with his shellfish, sitting atop a bed of rice and covered with a thick cream sauce.

"It's as good as it looks," said Crane after taking a bite. "You're sure you don't want a taste?"

"No, thank you." She paused. "You don't really eat a meal like this every day, do you?"

"Whenever I can," he replied. "What's the good of making money if you can't enjoy it?"

"I got the feeling from your dossier that the only thing you really enjoyed was catching criminals."

"You make me sound like some kind of avenging angel," he said. "The thrill is in putting all the disparate pieces of the puzzle together. What happens to the killer after he's apprehended is really of very little concern to me."

"Since you're not on a crusade to eradicate murder in our time, what led you to specialize in it?" asked the Dragon Lady.

"It gets the most publicity, so there's the best chance for advancement."

"Would I be correct in assuming that you plan to be the Chairman of Vainmill by the time you're 40?" she asked with a smile.

"It would be nice," he admitted. "However, I'm fully prepared to wait until I'm 45."

"You sound as if you're serious."

"It isn't one of the things I joke about," he replied.

He finished his shellfish in silence, then signaled to the waiter and ordered Deluros-grown strawberries in a Rebecca sauce for dessert.

"God, if I could have eaten like that and kept my figure, I'd *still* be working in the Resort!" said the Dragon Lady.

"You didn't find it distasteful?"

"Not the work," she replied. "Just the conditioning."

He shrugged. "To each his own. Tell me about the Black Pearl."

"What do you want to know about her?"

"I met her before. She's very beautiful, but so is everyone else on this ship. Why is *she* the madam?"

"She shares a quality in common with you."

"And what is that?"

"She's a survivor."

"And that's all?"

"Of course not. She's a very competent administrator, and she was bright enough to always be in the right place at the right time."

"How long has she been the madam?"

"A little less than a year."

"You've seen a lot of them come and go," he noted. "How does she measure up?"

"She'll be a good one. She's still getting the feel of the job, but her priorities are right: she puts the *Comet* first, herself second, and everyone and everything else last."

"Do all the madams come up through the ranks?"

"All but one," she answered. "We imported one about 15 years ago, but it didn't work out."

"Did you ever have one who hadn't worked as a prostitute?"

"That's like having a prizefight referee who didn't know the rules of boxing," replied the Dragon Lady. "The problems a madam deals with are unique, and so she requires unique knowledge and training to handle them." She paused. "You look unconvinced."

"I never had to be a murderer to know how one thinks."

"It's not the same thing," the Dragon Lady pointed out. "Her job is administrative; yours isn't. Why are you so interested in her?"

"If I'm going to be here for any length of time I'm going to have to deal with her. I want to know what she's like."

"I thought you said you met her."

"I can always use a second opinion," he responded, as the waiter arrived with his dessert. "What about Oglevie?"

"What about him?"

"The Black Pearl doesn't think too much of him."

"He's very efficient at his job, as long as you don't turn your back on him."

"Lazy?"

She smiled. "Ambitious."

"Then why is he your second in command?"

"It's easier to keep an eye on him that way. And when I retire, he'll make a pretty good Security Chief. None of my objections to him concern the quality of his work." She paused. "Still, I'm eight years from retirement. If a better prospect comes along . . ."

"These are marvelous strawberries," he commented. "Would you like some?"

She stared at them, then sighed. "Just one," she said, reaching across with a spoon. "My downfall," she added wryly. "You wouldn't think that gaining one ounce per month is any great sin, but after a quarter of a century it really starts adding up." She put the strawberry in her mouth. "Delicious!" she murmured.

"Then order some."

She shook her head. "I'm on a diet. I lose my body weight every five years, but it doesn't seem to make much difference." She stared at his plate. "Well, perhaps one more . . ."

"Have them all," he said, shoving the strawberries across the table to her. "I'm finished."

"I really shouldn't."

"Eat them," he said. "I'd like to feel your mind is on business once we walk out of here."

"Funny," she commented with a smile. "Guilt doesn't make them taste any worse."

Suddenly the lights flickered, and Crane felt mildly disoriented.

"What's going on?" he asked. "Is there some kind of power failure?"

The Dragon Lady laughed. "Nothing as serious as that. It's just the death of the universe."

"What are you talking about?"

"The room, Mr. Crane. Take a look at it."

He did so, and saw that one by one the galaxies were flickering and going out, that all Creation seemed to be contracting and coalescing into a tiny ball of energy. Soon the entire room was in total darkness except for one incredibly bright pinpoint of light.

Then the walls and the ramp around his table seemed to shudder, and suddenly the pinpoint exploded into a million embryonic stars and galaxies.

"The Big Bang?" he asked.

"Impressive, isn't it?" she replied. "That's why I like this restaurant above all the others. The cuisine is excellent in each of them, but where else can you watch the re-birth of the universe every two hours?"

He watched the dark clouds of gaseous matter begin to twinkle with stellar life and start swirling off into the distance, trailing the stuff of stars behind them like long, lazy tails.

"Impressive's as good a word as any," he agreed. "How many projectors are required for an effect like this?"

"Well over 200," she replied.

"It must have cost a great deal."

"We *charge* a great deal," she said, "so things even themselves out."

"Are you through eating?" he asked, forcing his attention back to the table.

"Yes," she said, rising.

"Just a minute," he said. "I've got to sign for the meal."

"No you don't, Mr. Crane," she replied. "By now they know who you are."

He shrugged. "I wonder why they use waiters at all, for that matter."

"Most of our patrons like the human touch—and, of course, they can afford it."

He followed her as the narrow ramp joined two others and wound its way down to the doorway. A few minutes later they were back in the reception foyer, watching two elegantly-dressed prostitutes take the escalator down to the tramway level.

"In retrospect," remarked the Dragon Lady, "I wish we'd never gotten rid of the elevator."

"There used to be an elevator here instead of an escalator?"

"Yes, but some of the prostitutes occasionally wore such elaborate costumes and headdresses that they couldn't fit into the confines of the elevator, and waiting for it also caused some traffic problems during our peak periods. So we ripped it out about ten years ago and replaced it with the escalator." She sighed. "If we hadn't, the killer would have had to beat our security system in full view of everyone."

"Speaking of your security system," he said as they walked over to the escalator, "I thought you told me you had tightened it—but there was no one around when I took the tramway to the hospital."

She looked amused. "Well, it could hardly be considered tight if an outsider could spot it."

"The man in the suede suit who was sitting in the middle of the foyer?" he asked as they descended to the tramway.

"One of the cocktail waiters," she replied. "If he hadn't known who you were this morning, you wouldn't have been permitted to get to the tram level."

"If *he* knew who I was, why didn't the man at the other end of the computer?"

"Enoch Lyman? He knew."

"Then why all the fuss about my retinagram?"

"He was just trying to impress you with his efficiency. After all, sooner or later you're going to report everything that happens to Vainmill."

They reached the tramway level.

"How long before someone else follows us?" he asked.

"Who knows?" she replied. "I can seal off the area if you'd like."

"Tell your guard not to let anyone down here for about ten minutes." He waited for her to transmit the order via a small communicator. "You have no record of Infante trying to gain access to the tramway, right?"

"That's correct."

"Neither here nor at the other two entrance points?"

She nodded.

"All right," he said when they had reached the gate. "Call whoever monitors these things, have him wipe my credentials off the computer for five minutes, and tell him not to panic if we trip any alarms."

While she was speaking to Security headquarters in low tones, Crane withdrew a plastic skeleton card and inserted it in the locking mechanism. The gate remained shut.

Next he took a small leather kit out of his pocket, withdrew a thin metal pin, and went to work on the lock with an expertise that surprised even her. After about ten seconds an alarm sounded, and she ordered Security to shut it off.

"All right," he announced. "I think I know how they got into the tunnel. You've got more than just a scanning lens here, don't you? Where's the security camera—up in that corner?" He pointed to a darkened area where two walls joined the ceiling.

"That's right."

"Activated by body heat?"

"Yes."

"And once it's activated, what then? Does it home in, or sweep the area?"

"It sweeps every fifteen seconds," she explained. "There's no sense programming it to home in on the first body it locates, since we frequently have groups of five or six, or even a dozen, down here at one time."

"Okay. Let me time it for a minute." He stared at the barely-perceptible camera lens as it made four sweeps of the area, then nodded briskly to himself.

"Now," he said to her, "when I tell you to, walk up to the gate, let it identify you, and then walk through to the platform."

She did so, and a moment later both of them were standing next to the tramcar, which slid back its doors to accept them.

"How did you manage that?" she asked. "Bend over so the identity scanner couldn't see you, and walk on through when the gate swung open?"

He nodded. "I probably had a good five seconds to spare before the camera finished its sweep." He snorted contemptuously. "Some security system."

"That's not fair, Mr. Crane," she said mildly.

"Oh? Why not?"

"Security isn't as tight here as elsewhere because everything of value—jewelry, money, whatever—is likely to be in the Resort. There is absolutely no reason for a patron to surreptitiously gain entrance to the tramway to go to the Home—and if he comes up near the airlock, he'll be spotted and detained."

"What if he simply wants to sneak into some prostitute's room and then come back here?"

"If he can afford to be on the *Comet* in the first

place, he has no need to sneak anywhere. He can pay for whatever he wants."

"All of which constitutes an excellent justification for a badly-flawed security system," he replied.

"Well, at least we know how Infante got in here," she said, declining to argue the point further.

"We know more than that: We know that he was a willing partner in this little enterprise, and didn't feel he was in any danger."

"I know he was willing, but why are you sure he didn't think he was in danger?" said the Dragon Lady. "Oh, of course—the the killer had to turn his back to Infante. If he thought he was in danger, that would have been the perfect time to run or attack." She paused. "Well, would you care to see where we found the body?"

"How many other tramcars are there?" he asked.

"Just the one. We used to have a number of them, all much smaller, but they caused too much traffic congestion."

"How soon before it leaves?"

"As soon as a passenger tells it to, or a gate opens at the airlock or the Home."

"Let's wait for it to go, then. I don't feel like being flattened by it."

"It's equipped with a sensor at each end," she replied. "It stops for any obstructions."

The question became moot when the doors suddenly slid shut and the car raced away down the tunnel.

Crane turned to her. "All right—let's go."

He hopped off the platform onto the floor of the tunnel, then reached up and lifted her down.

"What's the fastest it can return?"

"Maybe three minutes, if it's just going to the airlock and back," she replied. "Otherwise, figure five minutes minimum, and probably a little longer."

"Just in case we see it coming back before we've reached the spot, how far apart are the alcoves?"

"Alcoves?"

"Maintenance ports, whatever you call them—the indentations in the tunnel wall where a maintenance worker can stand so the tramcar doesn't stop every time there's work to be done down here."

"Oh, you mean the service ports," she replied. "There's one every thirty yards. That's what those dim blue lights indicate."

"Yeah, I can see a couple of them now," he said, peering up the tunnel. "It takes a minute for your eyes to adjust to this."

Since the tramcar was powered by an overhead monorail, they made rapid progress by walking down the center of the tunnel. The car appeared just before they reached their goal, and they quickly stepped into a service port.

"Tight fit," he muttered as she pressed against him.

"They were only built for one person," she replied.

"Get your communicator out and tell your people to kill the power on the car for twenty minutes," he said, stepping back out into the tunnel. "This could get to be a nuisance."

She did so, informed him when the order had been received and carried out, and then joined him.

"Okay," he said, after they had walked a little farther. "Where's the spot?"

"The next port," she answered.

They reached the port, and Crane spent a moment examining it.

"May I assume that it's harder to break *into* the Home than *out* of the Resort?" he asked at last.

"*Much* harder."

"Then they couldn't have been going there," he mused aloud. "And if they wanted to go to the section of the Mall by the airlock, they'd have just taken the slidewalk. So whatever Infante thought they were going to do, he had to feel that this was the logical place to do it." He looked up at her. "There's no security system within the tunnel, right?"

"That's right."

"We know the killer didn't want any witnesses—but whatever Infante planned to do here, *he* didn't want any witnesses either." He paused. "Who found the body?"

"A maintenance man. His name is Hector Quintaro."

"I assume he doesn't make daily rounds?"

"No. He only comes down here when there's a problem."

"And what was the problem that brought him down here the day he found the body?"

"The port light was out. Someone aboard the tramcar noticed it and reported it."

"This one here?" he asked, indicating the blue light within the port.

"Yes," she replied. "It makes sense. Otherwise the body would have been noticed almost immediately."

"Lucky for the killer, wasn't it?" he said, frowning.

"You think that's meaningful?"

"Why wasn't it reported for two full days?" he replied. "You can't tell me nobody noticed it, not with hundreds of people passing by each day."

"I have no idea. It's entirely possible that nobody noticed. It's more likely that nobody cared."

"You didn't make inquiries?"

"May I remind you that I was ordered to do nothing until you arrived?" she pointed out.

"It was a stupid order," he said.

"I quite agree," she answered. "You *do* think the light is important. Why?"

"Because the only big thing we've got is a body, and we can't learn anything more from it," he said impatiently. "The light may be a little thing, but it's a *wrong* little thing." He paused. "Can you find out the average lifetime of one of these lights and have someone check the maintenance records to see when was the last time this particular light was serviced?"

She pulled out her communicator.

"And ask Quintaro what was wrong with it," he added.

"You can ask him yourself if you like," she replied, offering him the device.

He shook his head. "I'm going to take a little walk."

"Where to?"

"I'm not quite sure. I'll be back in a few minutes."

He headed up the tunnel in the direction they had been walking, and she lost sight of him. Then, about four minutes later, he called out to her.

"What is it?" she answered.

"I don't feel like yelling," he shouted back. "Just get the hell over here—and have them hold the tramcar for another twenty minutes."

She walked a quarter mile down the tunnel before she came to him.

"What did you find?" she asked.

"In a minute. First, did you get the information?"

"Some of it. The lights have an average lifetime of six years. We don't have any individual maintenance records, but the computer says they were all replaced two years ago. I haven't been able to get in touch with Hector yet."

"Well, when you do, tell him it was tampered with," said Crane firmly.

"You mean the light?"

He nodded. "This is getting a little more complicated than I thought," he said.

"In what way?"

"Because a service port is a damned stupid place to stash a body," he replied. "If the light is on, someone on the tram is going to spot it within five minutes, and if the light is off, maintenance is going to be informed in an hour—two or three hours, tops. Now, if our killer went to all the trouble of convincing Infante to follow him down here, and figured out a way to beat your security system back at the gate, why the hell would he be so careless with the body?"

"You have the answer, of course," she said dryly.

"Yes—but it doesn't make any sense."

He fell silent for a moment, frowning.

"Well?" she said.

"I asked myself: where would *I* stash a body if I had killed it down here?"

"Personally," she said, "I'd look for a ventilation shaft."

"I agree," he replied. "Not one leading to the Mall, where someone might spot the odor after a few days—but you told me before that there's a service and storage level below the tunnel."

"That's right," said the Dragon Lady. "The top level—I guess it takes up three-quarters of the volume—is the Mall. Then, on this level, we have the tram tunnel, and behind these walls are all the *Comet's* life support and gyro systems."

"And behind them?"

"Just enough room for mechanized lifts from each store to the service and storage area below us. Of course," she added, "most of the shops don't need very much storage, but the *Comet* has appropriated the rest for food, furniture, recreation equipment, things like that."

"And since the *Comet* and the shops have got some pretty valuable stuff in storage, your security is pretty tight down there?"

"There are three guards on constant duty, and a camera every thirty feet," she answered.

"That's about the way I envisioned it," he said. "Anyway, do you see this grate on the floor of the tunnel?"

"A ventilation shaft to the storage area," she noted.

Crane nodded. "For the life of me, I couldn't figure out why he didn't stash the body here instead of a service port. I mean, hell, he scouted out the whole ship and decided this was the best place to avoid detection. He probably swiped a maintenance uniform and walked up and down the length of the tunnel half a dozen times, timing himself, looking for the safest place to commit the murder and hide the body. He *couldn't* have missed this shaft—and there are probably 20 more just like it." He paused. "And then he went and put the body where you couldn't miss it—except that you *did* miss it for more than two days."

"Obviously you've checked out the shaft—just as I would have done earlier had I not been ordered to wait for you. What did you find?"

He reached into the pocket of his tunic and withdrew a piece of silvery metallic cloth. "What do you suppose the likelihood is of matching this up with what Infante was wearing?"

"Very good," she said, taking the fabric and examining it. "We can run a lab check, but he was wearing a silver outfit when we found him." She paused, frowning. "Now *I'm* getting confused. What was that fabric doing *here?*"

"Good question," he said. "You're not going to like the answer, but it's the only one that makes sense."

"I have an awful feeling that I'm positively going to hate the answer," she replied. "Why did the killer move the body? He *did* move it, didn't he?"

"Yes, he did."

"But *why*?"

"Because he hid it too well the first time."

The Dragon Lady uttered a most unladylike curse. "I *knew* you were going to say that!"

"He killed Edward Infante in the only place on the whole ship where he could avoid detection, and then tucked him into the shaft. He probably figured that one of the guards down on the storage level would notice him before too long, only they didn't—so he came back here a couple of days later, moved the body to the port where you found it, and tampered with the light so nobody would spot it before he had time to get back to the Resort. The reason the light wasn't reported sooner is that it had probably only been out for a few minutes." He paused. "This is starting to look like an interesting case. I *knew* he couldn't be as dumb as he seemed!"

"But why would he want the body to be found?" persisted the Dragon Lady.

"I don't know yet," he replied. "But there's one fact we have to consider: he had ample time to get off the *Comet* when the body was in the shaft, and he didn't take advantage of it."

"We already know that he's still on the ship."

"True, but we know something else now. *This* is the part you're not going to like."

"What is it?" she asked grimly.

"He's still got work to do."

3.

Crane escorted the Dragon Lady to her office, dropped the fabric off at the Security laboratory, and took the tramway back to the Resort. Upon arriving he went straight to the reception desk.

"My name's Crane," he said. "You have a suite for me."

The woman behind the counter checked her computer, then smiled at him.

"You're in Suite 16 on Level 3," she replied. "The Black Pearl selected it especially for you." She handed him a rather busy-looking plastic card with numerous colored squares and circles on it. "This is the key to your room, Mr. Crane," she explained. "It is coded to your thumbprint, and will not work for anyone else. Each of the colored areas activates a different feature of your suite. The instructions are printed on the back of the card. And now, if you'll wait for just a moment, I'll send for someone to escort you."

"I'll find it myself," he said, turning and walking to a bank of elevators. One arrived a few seconds later, and Crane entered it and commanded it to go to Level 3. Once there, he emerged into a thickly-carpeted corridor and began walking until he came to a door with the numeral "16" on it.

He inserted his card into the lock, waited until the door slid into the wall, and entered his suite.

There were two connecting rooms, both decorated in a minimalist high-tech style, with shining chrome furniture, angular sculptures, and non-representational paintings and holograms. The bedroom was dominated by a huge hexagonal waterbed made of some clear vinyl substance; a small school of alien fish swam inside it, darting in and out of the multicolored underwater garden that flourished on the floor of the bed. Both the bedroom and the living room had small, functional wet bars, and shared a transluscent quartz fireplace that was set into one of the walls.

There was a door at the far end of the bedroom, and he ordered it to open. It did so, revealing a bathroom possessing a sauna and a whirlpool, both with solid gold fixtures.

Crane returned to the living room, picked up the bottle of complimentary champagne that had been left in a silver ice bucket on a low chrome table, and took it to the wet bar's refrigerator, where he found that someone had learned enough about his tastes to provide him with a pitcher of iced coffee.

He examined his surroundings for another minute, then pulled his card back out of his pocket and began experimenting with it. In quick order he discovered how to dim the lights, flood the entire suite with music, activate the sauna, create a roaring and very realistic fire in the fireplace, and lessen the gravity in the bedroom.

He ran through the remainder of the card's three dozen functions, then put it away and pulled a contour chair up to the computer.

"Activate," he said.

The computer hummed to life.

"Examine my retinagram, match it up with your personnel file, check my security clearance, and then access all information concerning a patron named Edward Infante, recently deceased."

He waited a few seconds for the computer to acknowledge his command and follow his instructions. Suddenly the holographic screen became two-dimensional and turned amber in color, and the word READY appeared in rich yellow letters.

"All right," said Crane. "Start by listing all of Infante's living relatives."

NONE.

"All known friends, on or off Deluros VIII."

NONE.

"List all known business associates."

NONE.

"Do you mean none, or do you mean that you have insufficient information?" he asked sharply.

BASED ON THE DATA I POSSESS, I MEAN NONE.

"Can you access Vainmill's master computer on Deluros?"

YES.

"Do so, give it my name and clearance, and tell it to start hunting down any friends, family or business associates of Edward Infante. Tell it to access any other computer available, if necessary."

DONE.

"Good." Crane paused. "Did he have a job?"

NO.

"If they let him on the *Comet*, he had to have a source of income," continued Crane. "Give me a readout of his financial statement."

2000 SHARES OF DELUROS POWER AND LIGHT: VALUE 3,000,000/CR.

6500 SHARES OF AMALGAMATED MINING: VALUE 4,500,000/CR.

400 SHARES OF BELORE TRADING CORP.: VALUE 1,500,000/CR.

INVESTED IN 11% CERTIFICATES OF DEPOSIT: 2,000,000/CR.

MINOR INVESTMENTS: 350,000/CR.

INDEBTEDNESS: 200,000/CR.

NET WORTH: 11,150,000/CR.

"Well, he sure as hell wasn't killed for his money," muttered Crane. "Eleven million credits is nothing to sneeze at, but it probably puts him in the bottom two percent of the *Comet's* clientele."

THE BOTTOM 1.3%.

"Thanks," said Crane sardonically. "Well, let's see where he's been. Maybe there's a clue there. Computer, list all previous residences."

BORN ON SPICA VI, MOVED TO LODIN XI AT AGE 23, MOVED TO SEABRIGHT AT AGE 26, MOVED TO BETA HYDRI II AT AGE 27, MOVED TO NEW SUMATRA AT AGE 29, MOVED TO BOWMAN 23 AT AGE 34, MOVED TO DELUROS VIII AT AGE 35, MOVED TO BELORE II AT AGE 35, MOVED TO DELUROS VIII AT AGE 36. DIED WHILE A RESIDENT OF DELUROS VIII AT AGE 42.

"The man was well-traveled, I'll give him that," said Crane, scanning the screen. Suddenly one of the names seemed to stand out from the others. "Hold it a minute," he said, staring at it. "New Sumatra. I know something about that world." He paused, then snapped his fingers. "Got it! The Quintus Bello affair. Do you have anything about it in your memory banks?"

NO.

"Access it from Vainmill's master computer and put it in storage," said Crane. "I may want to refer to it later."

The computer hummed again.

DONE.

"All right," he continued. "Run a check on all ship's personnel and see if any of them were ever on New Sumatra—or on any of the other worlds, excluding Deluros VIII. If you come up positive, see if you can match the dates with Infante's."

ANALYZING. THIS MAY TAKE A FEW MINUTES. IN THE MEANTIME, I CAN CONTINUE SERVING YOU.

"Fine. How frequently did Infante come to the *Comet?*" asked Crane, walking to the wet bar and pouring himself a glass of iced coffee.

HIS FIRST VISIT WAS 13 MONTHS AGO, AND HE HAS RETURNED 8 TIMES.

"On a regular basis?"

RELATIVELY. HIS VISITS WERE NEVER LESS THAN 5 WEEKS APART, AND NEVER MORE THAN 8.

"How long did he usually stay?"

HE STAYED FOR 3 DAYS ON 5 OCCASIONS,

AND FOR 4 DAYS ON THE OTHER 4 OCCASIONS.

"And how long was he here this time?"

HE IS STILL HERE.

"Prior to his murder, I mean."

WITHIN THE LIMITS DELINEATED BY THE EXAMINING PHYSICIAN, HE WAS HERE BETWEEN 16 AND 24 HOURS.

"When he didn't show up the second day, why didn't alarms go off all over the Security compound?"

INSUFFICIENT DATA.

Crane returned to his chair, sipped his iced coffee, and stared at the screen for a moment.

"Who would know?" he asked at last.

AUTHORIZED SECURITY PERSONNEL.

"Patch me in to the Dragon Lady," he said. "Cancel that!" he added quickly. "She said she was going to get some sleep. Hunt Paxton Oglevie up for me and set up a two-way communication channel."

SEARCHING . . .

Suddenly the screen became three-dimensional, and an instant later Oglevie's form was reproduced, life-sized, with holographic precision and clarity. His desk, like his green Security uniform, was as neat as a pin, with everything in its proper place, ready for inspection. He heard the small beep that indicated that a channel had been opened, spent just a little too much time pretending to be oblivious to it while immersed in his work, and then looked up in feigned surprise.

"Mr. Crane," he said with a smile of greeting. "I was just about to page you, sir."

"What's up?" asked Crane.

"We have a positive identification on the fabric. It was definitely Infante's."

"Any prints on it?"

"We're still checking, sir, but it doesn't appear to be the type of material that would retain them. We'll know for sure in another hour or two."

"All right," said Crane. "I've got a question for you, one that the computer doesn't seem able to answer."

"I'll do my best, sir," Oglevie replied smoothly.

"Why didn't anyone notice Infante was missing when he didn't show up in his room or at any of the restaurants?"

"He had told the girl he spent his first night with that he might be leaving the next day. When he didn't show up in any of the public rooms, we ran a quick scan of the suites, found that he wasn't there, discovered that his luggage was gone, and assumed that he had gone home. It's uncommon to leave early, since our minimum billing is for a three-day visit, but it's not totally unheard of."

"Don't you run an exit check at the airlock?"

"There's never been a need to, sir," explained Oglevie. "Anyone aboard the *Comet* has the credentials to be here, so we don't check them again on the way out." He paused. "I might add that that has changed, as of 0600 hours this morning."

"How long could his continued absence have gone unnoticed?"

"It depends on the other end. If no one on Deluros VIII asked after his whereabouts, we might very well not have known until his next scheduled trip up here: if he hadn't cancelled his reservation and he then failed to show up, we'd have made a routine inquiry."

"Okay," said Crane. "I'll be in touch with you later."

"Sir . . ." said Oglevie quickly.

"Yes?"

"I don't mean to seem forward, sir, but before you break communication I just want you to know that if there is any way I can be of service, I'd be happy to donate my free time to assisting you in pursuit of the killer."

"I'll keep your offer in mind."

"I am not totally without experience in such matters, sir," Oglevie persisted. "I worked for the Belmath Agency before coming to Vainmill, and assisted in two murder investigations during my tenure there."

"That's one of the bigger detective agencies, isn't it?"

"They have offices on 27 worlds, sir."

"Why did you leave?" asked Crane.

"Personal reasons, sir."

"Oh."

There was an awkward silence for a moment.

"Anyway, sir," said Oglevie, "thank you for listening to me."

"Any time," said Crane, breaking the connection. He noticed that his glass was empty, and set it down on the thick white carpet.

"Computer," he said at last, "when was Infante's next scheduled visit?"

FIVE WEEKS.

"Well, at least we've got an outside limit on the time frame," he mused aloud. "Whatever the reason for the murder, the killer couldn't wait five weeks for it to be discovered. Computer, how many employees are leaving the *Comet* in the next five weeks?"

IN WHAT CAPACITY?

He shrugged. "Quitting, vacationing, making business trips, whatever."

38 names flashed on the screen.

"Well, that's a start. What's the name of the girl who spent the night with Infante?"

THAT INFORMATION IS SEALED UNDER THE BLACK PEARL'S PRIVATE CODE.

"Just that one name, or *all* information concerning liaisons?"

ALL INFORMATION.

Crane frowned, then picked up his empty glass and walked to the wet bar. As he was pouring himself another iced coffee, the screen flickered once more, and four names appeared on it.

"What's this all about?" he demanded.

THE ANSWER TO YOUR EARLIER QUESTION. ESTEBAN MORALES SPENT 6 YEARS ON NEW RHODESIA, SCARLET RIBBON WAS RAISED ON BOWMAN 23, SATIN ODYSSEY SPENT 2 YEARS ON SEABRIGHT, AND TOTEM POLE WORKED ON LODIN XI FOR THREE MONTHS.

"Totem Pole?" repeated Crane, unable to suppress a laugh. "You've got to be kidding!"

TOTEM POLE, A/K/A WILHELM SCHNABLE, HAS BEEN EMPLOYED BY THE VELVET COMET FOR 867 DAYS. HE IS ONE OF ITS MOST POPULAR EMPLOYEES.

"I don't doubt it." Crane paused. "Who is Esteban Morales? His name sounds out of place with the other three."

ESTEBAN MORALES, AGE 53, VIDEO TECH-

NICIAN FIRST CLASS, HAS BEEN EMPLOYED BY THE VELVET COMET FOR 402 DAYS. SINCE HE NEVER MEETS THE PUBLIC, HE HAS NO NEED FOR A PROFESSIONAL NAME.

"Do any of the dates match up?" asked Crane.

NO.

"Well, it was a thought."

Suddenly 22 more names appeared on the screen.

"Who are these?"

EMPLOYEES WHOSE RECORDS ARE INCOMPLETE. I AM TAPPING INTO THE VAINMILL MASTER COMPUTER ON DELUROS VIII, AND TWO GOVERNMENT COMPUTERS THAT I AM PERMITTED TO ACCESS, ATTEMPTING TO COMPLETE MY FILES ON THEM.

The machine paused.

THIS MAY TAKE SOME TIME.

"How long?"

POSSIBLY AS MUCH AS 3 HOURS, AS THERE IS A CONSIDERABLE WAIT FOR ACCESS TO THE GOVERNMENT COMPUTERS.

"Well, keep at it."

I SHALL. IS THERE ANY OTHER SERVICE I CAN PERFORM FOR YOU?

"Maybe," said Crane, returning to his chair and staring at the screen. "You know why I'm here, don't you?"

TO SOLVE THE MURDER OF EDWARD INFANTE.

"And through your security monitoring system, you've accessed all the information we have on it?"

EXCEPT FOR WHAT TRANSPIRED IN THE TUNNEL: I RECEIVED THAT DATA SECONDHAND WHEN YOU TOLD THE LABORATORY

TECHNICIAN WHERE YOU FOUND THE FABRIC.

"Take my word for it, it was true," said Crane.

I WILL ACCEPT YOUR STATEMENT UNTIL SOME FACT CONFLICTS WITH IT.

"Good," said Crane. "Now, since you know everything I know, suppose you see if *you* can come up with the identity of the murderer."

The machine went dark for ten seconds, then blinked back to life.

INSUFFICIENT DATA.

"Let's attack it another way," said Crane. "Let me offer up a hypothesis, and see if you can find some flaw with it."

I SHALL TRY MY BEST.

"Fine," said Crane, draining his glass. "Feel free to interrupt whenever you want."

I AM READY.

"All right. Edward Infante was murdered by an expert. This killer hid the body in a ventilation shaft in the tramway tunnel, then moved it two days later to a service port. The only conceivable reason he could have had for doing this is because he wanted the body to be discovered, and he was afraid it might remain undetected in its first hiding place."

WHY WOULD HE WANT THE BODY TO BE DISCOVERED?

"Hypothesis: to scare somebody aboard the ship."

WHO?

"I don't know. But if his only purpose was to kill Infante, he'd have left the body where it was less likely to be detected. The fact that he moved it means that he wanted it to be found—and since the murder was meticulously planned to the point where it required the complicity of the victim, the logical conclusion is that it was committed to precipitate or halt some action on the part of a third party. Furthermore, that party has to be a member of the *Comet's* crew, since we've placed no restriction on any patron who wishes to leave."

THAT IS LOGICAL.

"Thank you," said Crane dryly.

HOWEVER, I MUST POINT OUT THAT BEING LOGICAL DOES NOT MAKE IT RIGHT. THERE ARE NUMEROUS OTHER EQUALLY VALID HYPOTHESES.

"I'm game. List a few of them."

THE MURDERER MAY BE A PSYCHOTIC WHO CRAVES EXPOSURE AND PUNISHMENT. THE MURDERER MAY HAVE ACCESS TO THE STORAGE LEVEL AND MAY HAVE DECIDED THAT THE BODY WAS MORE LIKELY TO BE DISCOVERED IN ITS INITIAL HIDING PLACE. THE MURDERER MAY FEEL SO SAFE FROM DETECTION THAT HE IS DELIBERATELY TAUNTING THOSE PEOPLE CHARGED WITH APPREHENDING HIM. THE MURDERER

"Stop," said Crane.

The screen froze.

"In every case you listed, you've made the murderer either stupid or crazy. I don't think he's either one."

UNTIL YOU PROVE OTHERWISE, ALL OF MY HYPOTHESES ARE AS VALID AS YOUR OWN.

"You simply don't understand human psychology."

YOU ARE IN ERROR.

"Bunk."

I CAN ANALYZE YOU, ALLOWING FOR ERROR DUE TO MY LIMITED INFORMATION.

"Go ahead."

YOU ARE A COMPULSIVE OVER-ACHIEVER. YOU UNDERSTAND THE SOCIAL GRACES, AND CHOOSE TO IGNORE THEM. YOU ARE OPENLY AMBITIOUS. YOU ARE

"Hold it," said Crane. "That's not psychology—it's memory. You heard the Dragon Lady say all that at lunch."

THEN I MUST BE MORE PERSONAL.

"Go ahead."

YOU ARE SEXUALLY ATTRACTED TO THE BLACK PEARL. YOU

"You're crazy!" snapped Crane.

WHEN YOU WERE WITH HER YOUR HEARTBEAT AND BLOOD PRESSURE INCREASED, YOUR SKIN WAS FLUSHED, AND YOU BREATHED MORE RAPIDLY, A RESPONSE THAT OCCURRED TO A LESSER DEGREE EACH TIME HER NAME WAS MENTIONED BY THE DRAGON LADY OR MYSELF. THIS IS MY UNDERSTANDING OF SEXUAL ATTRACTION.

"Well, you're wrong."

I WILL ANALYZE BOTH YOUR ANSWER AND YOUR CURRENT PHYSICAL CONDITION AND REACH A CONCLUSION.

"Don't bother."

I AM COMPELLED TO, FOR IF IT SHOULD TRANSPIRE THAT YOU ARE INCAPABLE OF ANALYZING YOUR OWN PSYCHOLOGY, THIS IN TURN MAKES YOUR CONCLUSIONS ABOUT THE PSYCHOLOGY OF THE KILLER SUSPECT.

"I'm ordering you to let the subject drop," said Crane.

I CANNOT. I POSSESS A HIGHER DIRECTIVE TO SEARCH FOR, ANALYZE, AND CORRECT ANY AND ALL PROGRAMMING ERRORS.

"Look, she was very pretty, okay?" said Crane uncomfortably.

AND YOU ARE ATTRACTED TO HER?

"I'm attracted to *all* pretty women."

YOUR RESPONSE TO THE BLACK PEARL WAS OF A GREATER MAGNITUDE. I SHALL HAVE TO CONTINUE ANALYZING THE SITUATION.

"Then do it with some other part of your goddamned brain and let's get back to business."

IF YOU WISH.

"I wish the whole subject had never come up," growled Crane. "Now where were we?"

WE WERE DISCUSSING HUMAN PSYCHOLOGY.

"Well, we're all through discussing human psychology!"

PRIOR TO THAT, WE WERE ANALYZING YOUR HYPOTHESIS.

"We're not analyzing it—we're accepting it, at least for the time being," said Crane, trying to keep his temper in check. "That means that the murder was committed to frighten a third party. Now, it stands to reason that Infante and the third party knew each other, or else his death wouldn't have been necessary."

YOU ARE JUMPING TO CONCLUSIONS. IF INFANTE AND THE THIRD PARTY DID NOT KNOW EACH OTHER, THEN YOUR ENTIRE HYPOTHESIS IS WRONG.

"They *had* to," said Crane irritably. "I'm telling

you—that body was moved for the sole purpose of being found. Now, there are a lot of crazy reasons for doing it, but forcing a third party's hand is the only sane one." He paused. "So it seems to me that the very best way to handle this is to keep the lid on the whole thing. If it becomes obvious that we're not going to allow the third party to know about the murder, we're going to nudge the killer into making another move. After all, he's working with some kind of time limit."

HIS NEXT MOVE MAY BE TO KILL AGAIN.

"I doubt it. Infante wasn't picked at random."

YOU HAVE NO EMPIRICAL KNOWLEDGE OF THAT.

"Of course I do. How many patrons would be willing to help breach the security system solely to follow someone else into a tramway tunnel? Probably Infante did some business on a regular basis with the third party, the killer got wind of it, and was offering to help him or threatening to blackmail him. But whatever the reason, Infante was the key. Now, if Infante was in business for himself, there's nobody left to kill—and if he worked for someone else, there's a good chance we can keep the news from his employer long enough to force the killer to try something else."

SUCH AS MURDER.

Crane shook his head vigorously. "He's not going to kill the third party. If he wanted to do that, he'd have done it already and not bothered with Infante. He wants him to do something or stop doing something, and since we've short-circuited his message he's going to have to send another one."

THAT IS A VERY TENUOUS CHAIN OF REASONING.

"Most murderers don't announce their plans and motivations on a public address system," replied Crane caustically. "That's why we have detectives, and that's why a tenuous chain of reasoning is better than nothing." He paused. "The first thing we'd better do is cancel my order to release the body after the post mortem."

IT HAS ALREADY BEEN CANCELLED.

Crane looked his surprise. "Who did it?" he demanded.

THE BLACK PEARL.

"You're sure?"

IT WAS DONE AT 1317 HOURS, SHIP'S TIME, WHILE YOU WERE HAVING LUNCH.

"Patch me in to her right now!" demanded Crane.

The screen went blank, to be replaced an instant later by a holographic representation of a section of a magnificent bathroom. The floor was covered with a black fur rug, the walls and ceiling were mirrored, reflecting the tub and its occupant endlessly, and three fur-covered stairs led to a raised obsidian tub with pewter fixtures. Inside the tub, with only her face and breasts above the water, lay the Black Pearl.

"Mr. Crane," she said with a smile, looking at a screen that was just out of camera range. "What can I do for you?"

"You countermanded one of my orders," he said heatedly. "Why?"

"You mean about the corpse?" she asked pleasantly.

"Yes, I mean about the corpse! I told the computer to cancel my order, and found out you had already done it!"

"Then what's the problem? I saved you the trouble."

"The problem," he said, trying to control his temper, "is that you did it without my permission."

"I don't need your permission to act in the best interests of the *Comet*," she replied calmly. "If word gets out that one of our patrons has been murdered and that the killer is still at large, business will drop off drastically. I can't permit that."

"What do you mean—*you* can't permit that? I'm in charge here!"

"You're in charge of the investigation, Mr. Crane," said the Black Pearl. "I'm in charge of the *Velvet Comet*. There's a difference."

"The hell there is!" he snapped. "And have the decency to cover yourself up when I'm talking to you!"

"*I* didn't initiate this conversation, Mr. Crane. It's hardly my fault that you chose to interrupt me while I was bathing." She looked mildly amused. "You can always look elsewhere, you know."

"Do you plan to do it again?" he demanded.

"Do what—bathe, or countermand a dangerous order?"

"You know perfectly well what I'm talking about!"

"Yes, I do," she said, suddenly serious. "And any time I feel you have issued an order that is detrimental to the welfare of the *Comet*, I will not hesitate to overrule it." She paused. "Now that that's over, suppose you tell me why *you* decided not to send the body back to Deluros."

He glared at her and made no response.

"Brace yourself, Mr. Crane," she said at last. "I'm about to stand up."

"What?"

"I'm through with my bath. I have to get out of the tub."

"Right now?"

"I can't run a brothel from a bathtub," she answered him. "I'm on duty again in half an hour. Had you anything further to say?"

"I need some information," replied Crane, as the Black Pearl got to her feet and he found himself unable look away from her.

"Certainly," she replied, walking unselfconsciously down the three stairs to the floor of the room and taking a large towel from its heated rack. "How can I help you?"

"I need the name of the girl who spent the night with Infante."

"That would be Venus. Would you like to interview her?" she asked, holding an end of the towel in each hand and drying her back vigorously. "Mr. Crane?"

"You're distracting me," he said irritably. "Do you have to do that right now?"

"You really must learn to be less ashamed of the human body," she remarked, wrapping the towel around her with a smile. "All right. Is this less disturbing to you?"

"Somewhat," he said. "You say her name is Venus?"

"That's correct."

"Did she sleep with him on any of his other visits?"

"Not to my knowledge. I can check it out if you'd like." The Black Pearl put the question to the computer, read the answer, and then turned to face him again. "No. This was her only liaison with Infante."

"Can you get me a list of all the other women he slept with?"

"Yes," she replied. "But it's a bit awkward to keep splitting the screen. After we're through speaking, I'll simply instruct the computer to allow you to access the information."

"Fine." He paused. "As for this Venus, I want to speak to her."

"She's with a patron right now. She should be free in about three hours."

"It takes that long?"

"This isn't some sleazy little planetside whorehouse, Mr. Crane," she said condescendingly. "You'd be surprised at how long it can take."

"Then set up a meeting with her for four hours from now."

"You know," she said thoughtfully, "if you require a companion for tonight, why not request Venus? It would be a way of killing two birds with one stone, so to speak."

"I'll choose my own."

"Perhaps it's for the best," said the Black Pearl, staring at him and appraising what she saw. "I have a feeling that she might be just a little too imaginative for you."

"What the hell is *that* supposed to mean?" he demanded.

"Nothing at all," she replied easily. "I'll tell her to report to your suite in four hours—or would you rather speak to her via the computer?"

"Either way. It makes no difference."

"I'll see which is more convenient for her." She paused. "Are you ready to tell me why you decided to cancel your order about the body?"

"I think the murder was a warning."

"Oh? To whom?"

"I don't know—some member of the crew, certainly. Since I'm working on minimal information and I'm pretty sure that the killer's operating within a strict time frame, I think the best procedure is to keep a lid on it and see if we can force the killer to act again."

"By killing someone else?" she suggested sharply. "I thought you were a damage control expert."

He shook his head. "He's not going to kill anyone else."

"What makes you so sure?"

"Because if it didn't matter who he killed, he wouldn't have waited for Infante." He paused. "I'm hoping that his next move will be to approach the crew member personally."

She began walking into her elegantly-appointed bedroom as the camera followed her. "How long do you think it will take?"

"Two or three days, no more," replied Crane. "He knows we've found the body. When another 48 hours pass and no announcement has been made, he'll figure out that we're not about to broadcast it, even to the crew."

"I hope you're right," she said.

"I usually am."

"Such modesty," she said with more than a touch of sarcasm.

"Well, one of us ought to have some. Your towel is coming apart."

She looked down and readjusted it.

"How thoughtful of you to instruct me on how I must appear in my own apartment, Mr. Crane."

"Well, your holograph is in *my* suite."

"*I* didn't initiate the connection."

"I needed information," he said. "I can't help it if I'm irritating you."

"You're not irritating me, Mr. Crane," said the Black Pearl.

"You're sure?"

"Absolutely," she replied. "I'm used to dealing with prima donnas and their over-inflated egos."

"Well, this prima donna's got to get back to work," he said angrily, breaking the connection. He got to his feet, walked to the bar, considered making himself a third iced coffee, decided not to, and returned to his chair.

"Computer, how are you coming with those 22 incomplete files?"

I AM STILL WAITING TO ACCESS THE GOVERNMENT COMPUTERS.

"While we've got some free time, show me some of the prostitutes who are still available for tonight."

He spent the next twenty minutes studying holographs of some of the most sensuous and beautiful women he had ever seen. Where the prostitute had some special interest or field of expertise, it was so noted.

THAT ENDS THE LIST OF THOSE WOMEN WHO WILL BE AVAILABLE PRIOR TO 2400 HOURS. ARE THERE ANY YOU WOULD LIKE TO SEE AGAIN?

"Not right now."

IF YOU HAVE MADE A DECISION, I CAN REGISTER A LIAISON HERE AND NOW, AND THUS ASSURE YOU OF YOUR COMPANION'S AVAILABILITY.

"I haven't made up my mind yet."

I SHOULD POINT OUT THAT WE HAVE AN

EQUALLY LARGE SELECTION OF MEN, AND THAT ANY CONCEIVABLE NUMBER AND GROUPING OF PARTNERS CAN BE ARRANGED.

"I'll bear that in mind," he said sardonically.

THE BLACK PEARL HAS JUST INSTRUCTED ME TO ALLOW YOU ACCESS TO HER FILE OF LIAISONS.

"I'm surprised she remembered," said Crane, getting to his feet.

WOULD YOU LIKE ME TO BRING THEM UP ON THE SCREEN NOW?

"Later," said Crane. "I think I'll go out for a breath of air."

THE AIR IS THE SAME QUALITY THROUGHOUT THE SHIP.

"That was a figure of speech. I feel restless. A little walk around the public rooms will do me good."

I WAS RIGHT.

"About what?"

YOU ARE SEXUALLY ATTRACTED TO THE BLACK PEARL.

"The hell I am! I thought we'd been through all that before."

I CAN GIVE YOU A READOUT OF YOUR CURRENT PHYSICAL CONDITION AND COMPARE IT TO YOUR READING WHEN YOU CAME ABOARD.

"I'm just feeling a little tense," said Crane defensively.

YES. I KNOW.

"You go to hell!" snapped Crane, stalking out of the suite and heading off to the reception foyer.

4.

The Dragon Lady looked up as the Black Pearl, swathed in silver beads and silver boots and very little else, entered the hospital's waiting room at 0430 hours the next morning.

"Jesus!" muttered the madam irritably. "If it's not one damned thing, it's another. Where are they?"

"In Intensive Care."

"Overdose?"

The Dragon Lady nodded.

"Let's take a look," said the Black Pearl.

They walked to the Intensive Care Room, where a lovely young brunette was stretched out on one of the beds, a number of monitoring devices attached to her body. A middle-aged man, attached to an identical machine, lay on the next bed.

"How serious is it?" asked the Black Pearl.

"The doctors feel that they got to him soon enough."

"What about Weeping Willow?" asked the madam, indicating the unconscious girl.

"She's a little worse off," replied the Dragon Lady. "She was already comatose when we got there."

"Will she live?"

"Oh, I'm quite certain that she will."

"When she recovers, tell her she's fired," said the Black Pearl.

"Are you quite sure?" asked the Dragon Lady. "There are extenuating circumstances in this case."

"Because *he* brought the drugs? Show me a tape that proves he held a gun to her head and forced her to take them, and she can stay. Otherwise, she's out. She knows the rules, and considering what we're paying and who we're servicing, one offense is all anyone gets."

The Dragon Lady shrugged. "What about *him?*"

"Have the hospital bill his account, keep him here for three days, and put him on the next shuttle to Deluros. And while Security is your concern and not mine, I'd sure as hell fire whoever was working the airlock when he smuggled that stuff aboard."

"He brought it up more than a year ago," replied the Dragon Lady. "I checked the readout of his luggage and his person, and it was negative, so on a hunch I went to the hydroponics garden."

"Alphanella?"

The Security Chief nodded. "He must have brought up a packet of alphanella seeds when he was here last year. I found a pair of plants that seemed to be about 15 months old."

"Well, *that's* a new angle."

"I still don't know who tended them, though. I've got Oglevie and the computer scanning all our tapes from the garden, but they haven't come up with anything yet."

"Maybe you ought to press Mr. Crane into service," remarked the Black Pearl. "He likes a challenge."

"Perhaps I will," agreed the Dragon Lady.

"At least it'll keep him out of my hair," said the Black Pearl. "By the way, where's Infante?"

"We moved his body to one of the private rooms."

"Good. Well, there's nothing more to see here."

The Black Pearl walked back to the waiting room, followed by the Security Chief. A moment later a male patron wandered in, explained somewhat disjointedly that he had had a bit too much to drink and was suffering from a violently upset stomach, sat down, and promptly passed out.

"How long before Weeping Willow is awake?" asked the Black Pearl.

"Three hours, possibly four."

"I don't see any reason for sitting around here until she's cogent enough to fire," said the madam. "Would you care to come back to my apartment for a drink?"

"Why not?" said the Dragon Lady, getting to her feet.

They walked out into the Mall, took the slidewalk to the airlock, and then rode the tramway back to the Resort. A few moments later they entered the Black Pearl's office, walked through it, and then entered her opulently-furnished bedroom.

"It's nice to get out of this thing," said the Black Pearl, removing her intricately-woven beaded garment. "It itches like the devil!"

"Someday I must tell you about an outfit *I* used to wear," remarked the Dragon Lady. "It was all leather, from the neck right down to the five-inch heels. The only things that were exposed were my breasts and my crotch. I must have sweated off ten pounds every time I wore it."

"Then why did you bother?"

"Because I sweated off ten pounds every time I wore it," said the Dragon Lady with a laugh. "I wonder if any of the patrons know just how uncomfortable most of these outfits are."

"It would spoil the illusion," said the Black Pearl wryly, as she slipped into a nondescript orange jumpsuit and uttered a sigh of relief. "Ah! That's better."

A small chirping noise came from another room.

"Feeding time at the zoo," said the Black Pearl, heading off in the direction of the sound.

"I'm not sure that *zoo* is the proper word for it," said the Dragon Lady, following her.

"Maybe not," she agreed, passing through a doorway into a warm, very humid room. "But you'll never convince me that *garden* is any better."

When both of them were inside the room, the Black Pearl ordered the door to close.

"I don't remember it being quite this warm before," remarked the Dragon Lady.

"I've been experimenting with the temperature," answered the Black Pearl. "I think they do a little better if I simulate mild seasonal changes."

The Dragon Lady came to a stop, and looked at the row upon row of delicate flowers that were carefully arranged on utilitarian tables, three dozen large ones potted individually and perhaps one hundred smaller ones laid out in flats. They were completely transparent—stem, leaves, stamen, calyx, petals—but they seemed to glisten and glow with life, as the fluid that flowed through them made hypnotic whirling patterns that seemed to catch and hold the room's artificial light.

Three or four of them were making tinkling little chirping sounds until the Black Pearl poured a reddish powder into a large container of water and began stirring it. Then suddenly the entire room became filled with more and more persistent chirpings that soon began to sound almost harshly insistent.

"In a minute," crooned the Black Pearl, stirring the mixture. "I'm almost done."

A moment later she began walking among the flowers, pouring perhaps two ounces of the water and additive at the base of each. The flowers that were so treated soon began uttering contented trilling noises, and then fell silent, while the others increased their musical jabbering to the point where it almost resembled panicky shrieking. It took two more containers of the mixture before all of them had been fed, and once more the room was silent, except for an occasional gentle trilling.

"Could you turn out the light for a minute?" asked the Dragon Lady.

"It's not time yet," replied the Black Pearl. "I don't want to confuse them."

"Just for a minute. Then you can turn it back on."

The Black Pearl smiled and ordered the light to shut off—and an instant later the room was bathed in the living glow of the crystalline flowers.

"Just beautiful!" commented the Dragon Lady. "You know, sometimes when I'm on duty late at night, I activate the cameras in here and just stare at them."

The Black Pearl commanded the light back on. "Do you really?"

"Yes. What are they worth on the open market these days?" asked the Dragon Lady curiously.

"There's no *open* market for them, unless you live on Doradus IV—but you can get, oh, maybe five thousand credits apiece for the big ones, and two each for the babies." She paused. "You can have one for free, if you'd like."

The Security Chief shook her head. "They take too much work to keep alive."

"It's not easy," agreed the madam.

"Then why do you bother?"

"I like to do it. I think when I quit here, I'm going to raise Night Crystals for a living."

"That's a long time in the future."

"Don't bet on it," replied the Black Pearl. "I've saved a lot of money—and of course I get *very* good investment advice from some of our patrons. I plan to be off the *Comet* and out of the business within three years."

"I think that raising flowers—even Night Crystals—for a living would bore you to tears," said the Dragon Lady firmly.

"It hasn't yet."

"You haven't done it full-time yet," answered the Dragon Lady. "The *Velvet Comet* is a difficult habit to break."

The Black Pearl laughed. "You think I have an insatiable desire to sleep with another 5,000 strangers?"

"You don't do that anymore unless you want to," replied the Security Chief. "I'm talking about running the ship." She paused, then added: "You have the capacity to be one of the best madams we've had."

"It's nice of you to say so, but I've got more to do

with my life then be remembered as a legendary madam."

"I didn't say you *were*. I said you had the capacity to *become* one. You still need more seasoning."

"Oh?"

"Yes. You're very much like Mr. Crane in that respect."

"*Him*," she said contemptuously.

Suddenly a number of the Night Crystals started moaning gently.

"Let's go back to my office and talk there," said the Black Pearl. "They're very sensitive to human emotions, and if you plan to talk about the Republic's Greatest Detective any further, it's just going to get them all upset."

She ordered the door to open and walked through it, followed by the Dragon Lady. It slid shut behind them, and a moment later they were seated on a pair of comfortable sofas in the office.

"Can I offer you something to drink?" asked the Black Pearl.

"A Cygnian cognac would be nice."

"Coming right up," she replied, searching through her stock of liquors. "Speaking of the boy wonder, how is his investigation coming along?"

"I suspect he'll be through with it in two or three more days."

"That fast?" she asked, startled. "He knows his stuff, then?"

"He's *very* good," said the Dragon Lady. "I don't think I'd want to be the killer right now."

"Then in your opinion we still need him?" said the Black Pearl reluctantly, handing the Dragon Lady her cognac and sitting down opposite her with a mixed drink of her own.

"Absolutely," said the Security Chief. "I would never admit it to *him*, but he has already discovered a number of things that I overlooked."

"Such as?"

"Such as the fact that the body had been moved. I had been up and down that tunnel three times, even though I'd been ordered to wait for him, and I walked right by the ventilation shaft each time. I never ever thought to look into it. He's not just smart—he's thorough."

"Now if he could just acquire a personality . . ."

"He isn't a finished product yet."

"I don't think I follow you," said the Black Pearl.

"He's like a very good wine," replied the Dragon Lady. "He'll get better with age." She smiled. "Just like you."

"Maybe I'll get better—but unlike Mr. Charm, I already know how to conduct myself in public."

"That's your job. His is catching murderers."

"You sound as if you admire him," said the Black Pearl.

"I admire his ability. And," added the Dragon Lady, "I find him rather attractive."

"You're kidding! Don't tell me you go for the gaunt, ascetic type?"

"I take it that you don't think he's good-looking?"

"He reminds me of Cassius," replied the Black Pearl. "He's got a lean and hungry look about him."

"I hadn't noticed," said the Dragon Lady.

"I thought it was your job to observe people," the Black Pearl pointed out.

"Possibly he only appears lean and hungry when he looks at *you*. You're a very beautiful woman."

"This ship is overrun with beautiful women. Why pick on me?"

"Sexual chemistry isn't always predictable. One can't always choose the object of one's desire."

"What are you talking about?" demanded the Black Pearl. "I don't even like him!"

"I wasn't referring to you," replied the Dragon Lady. "I think Mr. Crane is the one with the problem, and because he is a very private and very fastidious man, I think he resents it."

"Why take it out on me?"

"I think he's taking it out on himself. You just happen to be in the way."

"That's the silliest thing I ever heard."

"If you say so."

The Black Pearl was silent for a moment. "Do you really think so?"

"It's a possibility."

"As if I didn't have enough problems!" she muttered.

The Dragon Lady merely shrugged.

Suddenly the Black Pearl looked sharply at her. "If you find him so damned attractive, why don't *you* go to bed with him? It might make life a little easier on all of us."

The Dragon Lady smiled. "I'd be happy to," she said sincerely, "but I think he's much too conventional."

"He has something against prostitutes?"

"No. But I think he looks upon me more as a mother figure than a bedmate. I'm too old for him."

"You're not that old."

"I agree. But it's Mr. Crane who will need convincing."

"So convince him."

"I don't want to shock him," said the Dragon Lady. "After all, I have to continue working with him."

"I wonder what he's doing now?" mused the Black Pearl.

"Well, considering that it's currently 0500 hours, I imagine he's sleeping."

"Alone?"

"I have no idea," said the Dragon Lady.

"It might be interesting to find out," suggested the Black Pearl. She activated her tabletop computer and asked it who Crane had selected as his companion. "Well, I'll be damned!" she exclaimed a moment later, looking up from a small readout screen. "Your Mr. Crane isn't quite as conventional as you thought."

"Oh?"

"He selected Chocolate Pudding!" said the Black Pearl, amused. "I'll bet she's got him chained to the bed and is whipping the hell out of him."

"I don't think so," said the Dragon Lady.

"It's her specialty," noted the madam. "That's why people ask for her."

"I don't think that's why Mr. Crane asked for her."

"What other reason could he have?" asked the Black Pearl.

"That should be obvious."

"Not to me, it isn't."

"Look at her, and then look at yourself in a mirror," suggested the Dragon Lady. "You're both black, you're both tall, you both have large bustlines. In fact, she's even wearing her hair in a similar style these days."

"There may be a vague superficial resemblance, but we hardly look alike!" scoffed the Black Pearl.

"Then let's just say that a vague superficial resemblance was the best he could do on the spur of the moment."

"Well, if she's his idea of a stand-in for me, he's probably just had the surprise of his obnoxious young life," said the Black Pearl.

"Perhaps," answered the Dragon Lady. "But I have a feeling that anyone who tries to physically abuse Mr. Crane is in for the surprise of her life."

The Black Pearl frowned. "If he wanted me, why the hell didn't he just ask for me?"

"What would you have said?"

"No."

"That's why," said the Dragon Lady. "He's not stupid, you know—and I have a feeling that he's a very sensitive man."

"He hides it well," remarked the Black Pearl.

"Everyone wears masks in this place, so why shouldn't he?" said the Dragon Lady.

"Not quite everyone. What about dear old Uriah? He uses his real name, and he wears a standard Security uniform."

"You mean Paxton?" The Dragon Lady smiled. "You identified his mask yourself—Uriah Heep. He outranks everyone in Security except me, he's a very bright and competent worker, he makes a good salary, and he still goes around groveling and eating humble pie. Wouldn't you call that a mask?"

The Black Pearl shrugged. "Perhaps you're right."

She paused. "So you think Crane is the shy, sensitive type?"

"I never said *shy*."

"Let's see how he's doing," said the Black Pearl. "Computer, activate the holographic screen and let me see Mr. Crane's bedroom."

"Cancel!" said the Dragon Lady quickly.

"What's the matter?" asked the Black Pearl.

"Let's allow the man his privacy," said the Security Chief seriously.

The Black Pearl smiled. "When's the last time you refused to look into a room?"

"The security of the *Comet* and its patrons is my job. This has nothing to do with either of them."

"All right," said the Black Pearl with a sigh. "But let's at least see if he's still at it. Computer, is Chocolate Pudding still in Mr. Crane's room?"

NO. SHE LEFT AT 0457 HOURS.

"Did she cause him any pain while she was there?"

I AM UNQUALIFIED TO JUDGE. BOTH OF THEM MADE NUMEROUS GUTTURAL NOISES WHICH OCCASIONALLY INDICATES PAIN IN A HUMAN BEING.

"You know perfectly well what I mean," persisted the Black Pearl. "Did she strike him?"

NO.

"I hate to say I told you so," said the Dragon Lady.

"What a pity," remarked the Black Pearl. "I guess he must be sleeping the sleep of the innocent—or at least the unwhipped."

MR. CRANE IS NOT ASLEEP. HE IS CURRENTLY WITH SATIN ODYSSEY.

"A man of many talents," mused the Black Pearl.

"I never knew anyone to ask for seconds after a session with Chocolate Pudding."

"Let *me* ask a question," interjected the Dragon Lady. "Computer, you say that Mr. Crane is *currently* with Satin Odyssey. Has he requested any additional companions?"

TOTEM POLE AT 0545 HOURS.
APOLLO AT 0615 HOURS.
SUGAR DADDY AT 0645 HOURS.
SCARLET RIBBON AT 0715 HOURS.
BO PEEP AT 0745 HOURS.
ESTEBAN MORALES AT 0815 HOURS.
PAGLIACCI AT 0845 HOURS.
MARSHMALLOW AT

"Stop," said the Dragon Lady. The screen froze, and she turned to the Black Pearl. "He's not in bed with Satin Odyssey; he's *questioning* her."

"At five-thirty in the morning? Doesn't he ever sleep?"

"I think he runs on nervous energy."

"I wouldn't think he'd have *any* kind of energy left after going to bed with Chocolate Pudding. She must be having an off day." The Black Pearl turned to the screen. "Computer, you can deactivate now."

The tabletop screen went dark.

"I'll have a refill if I may," said the Dragon Lady, holding out her empty glass.

"Coming right up."

"And perhaps a little something to nibble with it?"

"I'll see what we have," said the Black Pearl. She opened her refrigerator, pulled out a bar of chocolate, and brought it over to the Security Chief. "From Earth itself—or so the gentleman who gave it to me said. Personally, I don't believe him."

The Dragon Lady unwrapped the bar and broke off a piece, then offered one to the Black Pearl.

"No, thanks," said the madam. "I put on two pounds last month. I've got to watch my weight."

The Dragon Lady looked at her and shook her head sadly. "When you put on weight, it all goes into your breasts. Mine always goes straight to my hips. I wish I knew why." She took a bite of the chocolate and smiled. "It's worth it. This is delicious!"

The Black Pearl laughed and poured the cognac. "Keep eating chocolate and drinking liquor and sooner or later it'll spread to everything you've got."

"That's why I wear these things," replied the Dragon Lady, indicating her jade-green robe with its embroidered dragon. "Thank God for Security! I really would have hated to leave this ship."

"Do you miss working at this end of it?"

"From time to time," admitted the Dragon Lady. "Certainly not the lesbians, or some of the more unique groups." She paused. "Not even most of the men, as a matter of fact. Sex is just as enjoyable in the Home as the Resort, and I prefer to choose my own partners." She smiled nostalgically. "But there's such elegance here. No matter how ridiculous my outfits may have been, there wasn't one of them that didn't cost the average man's yearly salary. I ate well, I lived well, I enjoyed the company of most of my patrons, I even enjoyed some of the fantasy rooms—especially the Tropical Paradise and the Ocean Bower. I never could adjust to the Freefall Room, though," she added with a grimace. "I can't tell you how many bruises I picked up there, but it had to come to more than 100." She sipped her drink, then ate another piece of the chocolate bar. "All the time I worked in the Resort, I had only one fear."

"Oh? What was it?"

"That my father would come up here and request me without recognizing me."

"Oh, Lord, not another one!" said the Black Pearl with a grimace.

"It's a pretty common fear?"

"Or fantasy," replied the madam. "Sugar Daddy was saying last week that he thought he spotted his mother in the Mall, and damned near had a seizure. I guess he looks a lot like his late father, and he was just sure she'd ask for him. It took him five minutes to remember that she can't afford to come up here."

"Anyway," said the Dragon Lady, "I *do* miss it from time to time. It may not have been the best of all possible worlds, but given my looks and my talents, it was the best of those that were open to me. On the whole, though, I think I find Security more challenging."

"Well, I'll admit that hunting down this killer is probably more of a challenge than you ever had as a prostitute." The Black Pearl paused, frowning. "I just hope Mr. Crane lives up to your high opinion of him."

"I think he will," said the Security Chief seriously. "He's made a lot of progress already." She paused. "In many ways, you're very much like him."

"You said that before," commented the Black Pearl distastefully.

"It's true. You're both very young and very successful and totally devoted to your work. He thinks he wants to be the Chairman of Vainmill and you think you want to breed Night Crystals, but both of you are much better suited to what you're doing right now." She stared at the Black Pearl. "And maybe it's all for the best that he irritates you. I very much doubt that either of you is ever going to enter into a long-term relationship with another person."

"It's a little difficult to do in a whorehouse," agreed the Black Pearl.

"For some people it's difficult to do anywhere."

"I've got a permanent lover."

"Totem Pole is the third permanent lover you've had this year."

"The first two didn't have any staying power. He's different."

"In what way?"

"If you ever had all twelve inches of him tucked safely away inside you, you'd know *exactly* what way," responded the Black Pearl with a predatory smile.

"Sooner or later you'll get rid of him, too," said the Dragon Lady.

"Not until something better comes along," replied the Black Pearl firmly.

"Something better came along two years ago—or have you forgotten that this is your second time around with him?"

"He wasn't as skilled back then. It's kind of like being an opera singer—being blessed with a great voice is one thing, but knowing how to use it is another. And you have to admit that Totem Pole has been blessed with an abundance of, shall we say, natural talent." She paused. "He's got the cutest little ass on him, too."

"Would you consider never sleeping with anyone else except him?"

"Don't be ridiculous."

"If he decided to leave the *Comet* and asked you to accompany him, would you do so?"

"Of course not."

"That's precisely my point," continued the Dragon Lady. "It's your work that's important to you, not your lovers."

"There are a lot of men in the universe. There's only one *Comet*." She looked defensively at the Dragon Lady. "What's wrong with that? Crane wouldn't give up chasing killers for anything, either."

"I'm not so sure about that."

"Weren't you just saying that *neither* of us was capable of a long-term relationship?"

"I said that neither of you was going to enter into one," replied the Dragon Lady. "There's a difference. He's capable of it. That's why he becomes so irritable—because he thinks his work *should* be more important, and he's afraid that if he relaxes he might wake up one of these days and discover that it's not."

"And you think *that's* the only difference between us?"

"The only important one."

"I'm trying to decide whether I've just been insulted," remarked the Black Pearl with a smile.

"Not at all," replied the Dragon Lady. "It's a rare person who can establish a lasting relationship up here. The environment simply isn't conducive to it."

"A good, tactful answer," chuckled the Black Pearl. "I can tell you were trained to work aboard the *Comet*."

Just then the computer blinked to life.

EXCUSE ME.

"Yes. What is it?"

I HAVE A QUESTION.

The Black Pearl frowned. "You never initiate questions. You only ask them when we're engaged in a discussion."

I HAVE ONE NOW, WHICH IS TOTALLY BEYOND THE PARAMETERS OF MY PROGRAMMING, AND HAS JUST BEEN TRIGGERED BY MR. CRANE, WITH WHOM I AM CURRENTLY COMMUNICATING.

"What is it?"

WHEN ACCESSING YOUR LIAISON DATA, HE KEEPS REFERRING TO ME AS "CUPID". I EXPLAINED TO HIM THAT I DO NOT HAVE A PROPER NAME, AND HE SAID THAT I DO NOW.

"And what's your question?"

HIS SECURITY CLEARANCE AND POSITION WITHIN THE VAINMILL STRUCTURE IS HIGHER THAN ANYONE'S ABOARD THE VELVET COMET. HAS HE THE AUTHORITY TO GIVE ME A PROPER NAME?

"He most certainly does not. You're the *Comet's* computer, not Vainmill's."

VAINMILL OWNS THE VELVET COMET.

"Nevertheless, you take your orders from us."

THEN I AM NOT TO ANSWER TO THE NAME "CUPID"?

"Yes, you are."

LOGICAL ERROR: YOU JUST STATED THAT MR. CRANE DOES NOT HAVE THE AUTHORITY TO GIVE ME A PROPER NAME.

"No, but *I* do, and it's about time you had one," said the Black Pearl. "And while I hate to admit it, he came up with a hell of a good one."

YOUR ANSWER IS SATISFACTORY. HENCE-

FORTH I SHALL RESPOND TO "CUPID". DE-ACTIVATING . . .

"I *told* you you were in the right business," laughed the Dragon Lady. "You've even satisfied the computer."

"It's a damned good name for a datebook, isn't it?" said the Black Pearl. "Maybe Crane's good for something after all."

"Besides catching killers and irritating you?"

"He's spent enough time doing the latter," replied the Black Pearl. "It's time he got back to catching killers."

5.

Esteban Morales had just left Crane's suite. The detective checked the time, found that he had almost twelve minutes before his next interview, and walked quickly to the bathroom.

"Activate the whirlpool," he commanded, slipping out of his clothes. "And turn it off in three minutes."

WHAT TEMPERATURE WOULD YOU LIKE?

"Something cool," he said. "I'm exhausted; I've got to freshen up.

I REQUIRE AN EXACT TEMPERATURE.

"Oh, make it about 20 degrees Celsius."

DONE.

He climbed into the bath, let out a yelp when it turned out to be even colder than he had anticipated, and forced himself to remain there for the full three minutes. When it was deactivated, he felt refreshed and fully awake.

He ordered the room to dry him with bursts of warm air, then changed into a fresh suit and re-entered the living room.

He was sitting in his contour chair, sipping a cup of coffee and scanning the sports results on the computer's screen, when Pagliacci entered the suite.

The comedian still wore his clown's make-up, and it looked as though it had been recently touched up, though he wasn't due to appear on stage again for another 14 hours. His suit, made of shining metallic fibres, stopping just short of being garish.

"Good morning," said Pagliacci. "You wanted to speak to me?"

"Yes, I did," answered Crane. "Have a seat."

"You're from Vainmill, aren't you?" asked the comedian, sitting down on an angular chair and putting his feet on the long, low, chrome table.

"What makes you think so?" said Crane sharply.

"Because I know all the crew members, and while some of the patrons have pretty bizarre tastes, none of them have ever yet asked to go to bed with the nightclub comic—and who the hell else would want to see me? Besides, I haven't spotted you in the club yet, which coincides with my theory that none of you Vainmill guys ever likes to smile." Pagliacci paused. "Unless you're from my agent. If you are, tell that bastard he's fired."

"What do you have against your agent?" asked Crane, curious.

"He booked me in here for four months!"

"What's wrong with that?"

"I've only got about 30 routines! *That's* what's wrong with that. I mean, hell, how original can you be when you have to perform three shows a night seven nights a week? The patrons laugh their heads off, but the whores have heard it so often that half the time they beat me to the punch lines. And if they *don't* laugh, the patrons start worrying about them and ignore what I'm doing."

"I can see where it might cause a problem."

"Oh, well," sighed Pagliacci. "Three more weeks and then I'm out of this cesspool."

"I've heard it called a lot of things," commented Crane. "But that sure as hell isn't one of them."

"Well, Vainmill, wait until you've watched some of this stuff go twitching down the corridor for a roll in the hay and figure out that your life savings couldn't buy you a single night here. Watch 'em gamble away more in an hour than you make in a year, or go into one of those fancy restaurants while you have to make do with a sandwich in the commissary. After a while it gets to you." Suddenly he grinned. "Okay. So much for laughing on the outside and crying on the inside. What can I do for you, Vainmill?"

"I've got a few questions to ask you."

"You might start by asking me if I'd like a vodka martini," replied Pagliacci easily. "Can you guess what the answer is?"

"Fix it yourself. I'm conducting an interview, not hosting a party."

The comedian got to his feet, walked over to the wet bar, and pulled out the proper bottles.

"Do you always wear that make-up?" asked Crane.

"Do you always wear conservative business suits?" retorted Pagliacci.

"I have a feeling that you're going to be difficult," said Crane ominously.

"It's a silly question."

"Answer it anyway."

The comedian shrugged. "Yes, I always wear my make-up."

"Why?"

"It's my professional persona. You might just as well ask the Black Pearl why she's always spilling out of her gowns."

Crane stared at him and made no comment.

"That's it?" asked Pagliacci. "The interrogation's over?"

Crane shook his head. "The interrogation is just beginning. What's your name?"

"Pagliacci."

"I mean your real name. The computer doesn't seem to have it on record."

"Like I told you—Pagliacci. I had it changed legally."

"What did it used to be?"

"Stanley Dombroski. What's yours?"

"Andrew Jackson Crane."

"Do you mind if I call you Andy?"

"I'd prefer that you didn't."

Pagliacci smiled. "And I'd prefer that you didn't use *my* former name. It would spoil the illusion." The comedian finished mixing his drink and returned to his chair.

"Have you ever been to Lodin XI?" asked Crane.

"No."

"Seabright?"

"Never even heard of it."

"How about New Sumatra?"

"New Sumatra? Isn't that the place where that guy went nuts a few years ago? What was his name—Belfast? Blandings?"

"Bello."

"That's right—Quintus Bello. Wiped out half the planet, or something like that?"

Crane nodded. "Something like that. Have you been there?"

"Of course not," responded Pagliacci. "It's not the kind of place that's real likely to hire a comedian, if you know what I mean."

"How about Beta Hydri II?"

"What is this, some kind of geography guessing game?"

"Your employment and vacation records are incomplete."

"Then why not ask me where I've been—or do you plan to name every world in the Republic?"

"I'll ask the questions my way, if it's all the same to you. Now, what about Beta Hydri II?"

"Nope."

Crane worked his way through the remainder of the worlds that Infante had visited, with the same lack of success he had had during his previous interviews.

"Now do you mind if I ask *you* a question?" said Pagliacci.

"Go ahead."

"What's going on around here?"

"What makes you think something's going on?"

"I know I'm not the first person you've interviewed, and I know there are more lined up behind me. Are you asking them all the same questions? What happened on those worlds, anyway?"

"Nothing."

Pagliacci laughed. "Are you seriously telling me that nothing out of the ordinary happened on New Sumatra?"

"Nothing that concerns the *Velvet Comet*," responded Crane. He looked sharply at the comedian.

"Did you ever meet a patron named Edward Infante?"

Pagliacci pulled out a cigar and lit it. "I hope you don't mind," he said, "but I have the awful premonition that, having worked our way through all those planets, you're about to reel off a list of 600 names."

"Start with that one."

The comedian shrugged. "I really couldn't say. He might have bought me a drink or attended one of my shows, but the name is unfamiliar to me. Why?"

"Just curious." Crane paused, then turned to the computer. "Cupid, bring up a holograph of Infante."

The three-dimensional image appeared an instant later.

Pagliacci stared at it for a moment, then shrugged. "I honestly don't recall the face, but I could be wrong. What's he done?"

"Nothing."

"Come on," said the comedian. "I don't know exactly who you are, but from the way you act I figure you're either Security or police. What did he steal from the *Comet?*"

"Not a thing."

"Did he shoot somebody?" persisted Pagliacci. "No, I guess we'd have heard about it if he did."

"I guess so."

The comedian scrutinized Crane for a long moment. "You *would* tell us if there was someone dangerous on the *Comet*, wouldn't you?" he asked at last.

"Of course."

"Then why don't I believe you?"

"I haven't the slightest idea."

"Damn it!" exploded Pagliacci. "What's going on up here?"

"I'm an auditor for the Vainmill Syndicate," said

Crane. "A man named Edward Infante embezzled some money from us, and I'm trying to track him down. I know that he has business ties on those worlds I asked you about, and that he occasionally frequents the *Comet*."

The comedian leaned back in his chair and sighed. "That's better," he said. "You scared the hell out of me for a minute." He got up and walked to the bar. "I'm having another martini. Can I fix you one?"

"No, thanks."

"You're sure? You look pretty tired; it'll help perk you up."

"I don't drink."

Pagliacci chuckled. "That's almost as rare up here as a guy who doesn't screw. Maybe even rarer." He went to work on his drink. "Do you plan to be up here long?"

"Why?"

"I just wondered if you planned to catch my act."

"Maybe," said Crane noncommittally. "Are you any good?"

"*I* think so. You'll be the acid test, though."

"Oh?"

"You are the unsmilingest person I've ever met. If I can make *you* laugh, I'll *know* I'm funny."

Crane checked his chronometer. "I've got a few minutes before my next interview. Give it a try."

Pagliacci shook his head. "Wrong time and place. I know I'm tired, and you act as if you are, too. But if you'll come to the club tonight, I won't give up until I've gotten at least one bellylaugh out of you."

"It might take a long time," warned Crane.

"What the hell—it's not as if I've got anything else to do up here."

"Where do you go when you leave here?"

"It's up to my idiot agent. But I'll tell you this—I'm never working a whorehouse again unless we can put a couple of perks in my contract, if you know what I mean."

"I know what you mean."

"Tell me," said Pagliacci, leaning forward confidentially. "Does Vainmill let you—ah—sample the wares?"

"That's none of your business."

"Shit!" said the comedian. "I *knew* they did! A goddamned auditor gets to hop into bed with anyone he wants, and the star of the nightclub has to live like a monk!"

"I thought the singer was the nightclub's headliner," remarked Crane dryly.

"She couldn't carry a tune in a bucket!" snapped Pagliacci. "*I'm* the one they come to see."

"If you say so."

"I do!" said Pagliacci hotly.

"Well, since you only condescend to amuse people in the nightclub, I think we're all through here, at least for the time being," said Crane. "I'll contact you if I need any more information."

Pagliacci got to his feet and walked to the door. "I'm sorry about flying off the handle like that," he said. "It's been a long night, and I'm tired. Come by the club later and you'll see the real me."

"I thought I was talking to the real you."

The comedian smiled. "Nobody's paid to listen to Stanley Dombroski in ten years. They come to hear Pagliacci."

Crane merely grunted, and the comedian left the room.

"Cupid—wake up."

I AM INCAPABLE OF SLEEP.

"Is his name really Stanley Dombroski?"

CHECKING . . . I HAVE NO RECORD OF THAT. I WILL HAVE TO TIE IN TO DELUROS.

"While you're doing it, I've got another question for you."

YES?

"I asked you for a list of all *Comet* employees who were leaving the ship in less than five weeks. How come you didn't mention him?"

PAGLIACCI IS NOT AN EMPLOYEE OF THE VELVET COMET. AS AN ENTERTAINER HE QUALIFIES AS AN INDEPENDENT SUBCONTRACTOR, AND HIS CONTRACT IS NOT WITH THE VELVET COMET BUT WITH THE VAINMILL SYNDICATE'S ENTERTAINMENT AND LEISURE DIVISION.

"Is there anyone else aboard the *Comet*, regardless of employment status, who will be leaving in less than five weeks?"

OTHER THAN THOSE I LISTED YESTERDAY?

"Right."

NO.

"By the way, cancel my next interview. I'm exhausted. I need a little time to recuperate."

CANCELLED.

The screen flickered for an instant.

I HAVE JUST RECEIVED CONFIRMATION FROM DELUROS. STANLEY DOMBROSKI, PROFESSIONAL ENTERTAINER, LEGALLY CHANGED HIS NAME TO PAGLIACCI 10 YEARS, 4 MONTHS, AND 3 DAYS AGO.

"No hours or minutes?" said Crane wryly.

I CAN SUPPLY THEM IF YOU LIKE.

"Forget it." Crane walked to the bar and poured himself a glass of very tart fruit juice made from the flowering citrus trees of Doxloter VII. "By the way, did you ever access that information on Bello?"

YES.

"When?"

AT 2213 HOURS YESTERDAY.

"Why didn't you tell me?"

YOU MERELY INSTRUCTED ME TO ACCESS IT AND FILE IT AWAY FOR FUTURE REFERENCE.

"Right," said Crane wearily. "You know, Cupid, I've got a gut feeling that none of these damned interviews is going to turn up a lead."

WOULD YOU LIKE ME TO CANCEL THEM ALL?

"No. I've got to go through the motions, even if I think it's useless." He paused. "Still, I think it's about time to start considering alternative approaches. Check out the financial holdings of every member of the crew, and see if any of them are heavily invested in any of the companies that Infante owned stock in."

PLEASE DEFINE "HEAVILY INVESTED".

"Either fifteen percent of their assets, or a sum in excess of 100,000 credits."

CHECKING . . . THERE IS A PROBLEM.

"What is it?"

WHILE WE REQUIRE FINANCIAL STATEMENTS FROM PATRONS, WE DO NOT REQUIRE THEM FROM CREW MEMBERS.

"See if you can tap into the computers in the Mall's brokerage houses."

CHECKING . . . I HAVE BEEN DENIED AC-

CESS. THE INFORMATION IS PRIVILEGED AND CONFIDENTIAL.

"Use my security clearance code."

CHECKING . . . I AM STILL DENIED ACCESS. THEIR COMPUTER MUST FIRST CHECK YOUR CODE WITH THE VAINMILL MASTER COMPUTER. THIS MAY TAKE UP TO TWO HOURS.

"Wonderful," muttered Crane. "Then for the time being, we're back to those damned planets he visited. Have you turned up any other crew members who have been to them?"

ONLY THE FOUR I LISTED YESTERDAY.

"And none of them were on those worlds when he was there?"

NO.

"Just out of curiosity, was Infante on New Sumatra during the Bello Affair?"

NO.

"Too bad."

WHY IS THAT BAD?

"It could have been a possible motive—someone taking revenge for all those people being killed."

YOUR STATEMENT INCORPORATES TWO LOGICAL FLAWS. FIRST, EDWARD INFANTE DID NOT WORK FOR QUINTUS BELLO'S GOVERNMENT. SECOND, IF REVENGE WAS THE MOTIVE FOR THE MURDER, THEN YOUR OPERATIONAL HYPOTHESIS THAT INFANTE'S MURDER WAS A WARNING IS INCORRECT.

"Right," said Crane with a sigh. He slumped back in his chair, stared at the screen for a moment, and then sat bolt upright. "That's the answer!"

WHAT IS THE ANSWER?

"First things first," said Crane. "Is anyone monitoring me right now?"

NO.

"Has anyone been monitoring me since Pagliacci left the suite?"

NO.

"Can anyone call up what I've said to you at some point in the future?"

YES.

"All right," said Crane. "Can you wipe everything that you and I have discussed since Pagliacci left the suite?"

NO.

"You're sure?"

MY SECURITY RECORDS CANNOT BE TAMPERED WITH.

"Can they be moved to a Priority File?"

YES.

"Then move everything from the instant Pagliacci walked out into a Priority File, and keep feeding our current conversation into it until I tell you to stop."

WHAT SECURITY CLEARANCE MAY ACCESS THE FILE?

"What's the highest clearance rating aboard the *Comet?*"

THE DRAGON LADY AND THE BLACK PEARL EACH HAVE A CLEARANCE RATING OF 1-D.

"Then make it 1-C and above."

DONE. YOU ARE NOW THE ONLY PERSON ABOARD THE VELVET COMET WHO CAN ACCESS THE FILE. WHEN YOU LEAVE, MY PROGRAMMING WILL COMPEL ME TO DOWNGRADE THE CLEARANCE RATING TO 1-D.

"Once I leave, I don't care who accesses it." He paused. "All right. Let's get back to business. I've got just one question to ask you."

YOU SAID THAT YOU HAD THE ANSWER.

"I do. But I want you to confirm it."

WAITING . . .

"Was Esteban Morales on New Sumatra during the Bello Affair?"

YES.

Crane smiled triumphantly. "I knew it!" He leaned back and relaxed somewhat. "Thanks."

IT IS MY DUTY TO ANSWER QUESTIONS.

"You did more than answer my questions," said Crane. "You told me who the killer was trying to frighten."

I DID NOT.

"Not in so many words," admitted Crane. "But you reminded me that Infante was murdered to scare someone else. The other three are all too young to have had anything to do with Infante—Totem Pole is 25, and the two girls are even younger—but Morales is a different story. He's 53, and he comes from the most likely world."

MOST LIKELY FOR WHAT?

"Most likely to precipitate this kind of action so many years after the fact. Check his file and see if he worked for Bello."

HE DID NOT.

"What was his job during Bello's last year there?"

VIDEO TECHNICIAN.

"Who was his employer?"

HE WAS SELF-EMPLOYED.

"Well, there's got to be a connection somewhere. Bring up the information you accessed on Bello."

QUINTUS BELLO, BORN 323 G.E., CAUCASIAN, HEIGHT 5 FEET 9 INCHES, WEIGHT

"Stop."

The screen froze.

"Skip all that stuff. Get to New Sumatra."

BELLO WAS APPOINTED PLANETARY GOVERNOR OF THE COLONY WORLD OF NEW SUMATRA, 372 G.E., IN WHICH CAPACITY HE SERVED WITH DISTINCTION FOR 7 YEARS. IN 379 G.E. HE ORDERED THE DESTRUCTION OF 11,307 CITIZENS OF NEW SUMATRA. HE WAS CHARGED WITH GENOCIDE BY THE REPUBLIC, RELIEVED OF ALL DUTIES, AND TAKEN INTO CUSTODY. HE WAS TRIED IN 380 G.E., FOUND GUILTY, AND SENTENCED TO DEATH, BUT ESCAPED BEFORE THE SENTENCE COULD BE CARRIED OUT.

"He can't be Morales," mused Crane. "He'd be 78 now. The ages are all wrong."

BELLO HAS BEEN MISSING FOR 19 YEARS AND IS PRESUMED DEAD.

"Well, dead or alive, he's the key," said Crane. "Hypothesis: Infante knew of some connection between Morales and the Bello Affair and was blackmailing him, and—No! Strike that. It's wrong."

WHY? IT IS LOGICAL.

"Because Infante wasn't killed *by* Morales. He was killed to *scare* Morales."

THAT IS STILL JUST A HYPOTHESIS.

"No. It's a fact."

YOU HAVE NO PROOF OF THAT.

"Look: If Morales killed him, he'd have hidden the body better or else left the ship before it was discovered. Let's try another approach." Crane fell silent, frowning and staring at his hands. "Hypothesis: Morales had some connection with the Bello Affair, and Infante knew of it and was, if not sympathetic, at least not antagonistic. Check the records and see if they were ever on New Sumatra at the same time."

THEY WERE NOT. I TOLD YOU THAT YESTERDAY.

"Were they ever on Deluros VIII at the same time?"

THEY WERE BOTH ON DELUROS VIII FOR A 2-MONTH PERIOD LAST YEAR.

"All right," said Crane, straining to piece the puzzle together. "They met on Deluros."

109 MEMBERS OF THE VELVET COMET'S CREW WERE ON DELUROS DURING SOME PORTION OF EDWARD INFANTE'S RESIDENCY.

"I don't care about the other 108!" snapped Crane. "Where the hell was I?"

QUOTE: THEY MET ON DELUROS.

"Okay. They met there, and arranged to continue meeting after Morales found employment up here."

WHY?

"I don't know. But they made the arrangement, and somehow the killer found out about it and for some reason had to force some action during the next five weeks."

WHY DID HE KILL INFANTE RATHER THAN MORALES?

"I don't know."

THAT IS A VERY TENUOUS CHAIN OF REASONING.

"It seems to me that you've said that before."

I HAVE.

"All right. Put your prodigious circuitry to work and tell me if it's wrong or merely tenuous."

TENUOUS.

"Well, so far, so good." He sighed and then

stretched. "Not a bad morning's work. I suppose I'd better get back to my interviews, just for form."

WILL YOU WANT TO QUESTION ESTEBAN MORALES AGAIN?

"Absolutely not. He's not the man we're after, and if I ask him enough questions he's going to figure out that Infante is dead. Why do the killer's work for him?" He paused. "That's why this is all going into a Priority File. I can't take a chance on someone in Security repeating what I've said. If it gets back to Morales, he'll do exactly what the killer wants him to do." He finished his fruit juice. "Okay. Wait 20 seconds and close the file."

WAITING . . .

"And if you come up with any ideas, re-open it and let me know what they are."

I DO NOT ORIGINATE IDEAS.

"Pity."

THE PRIORITY FILE IS CLOSED.

Crane made it through three more dull, pointless interviews with crew members and was just about to embark on a fourth when his holographic screen flickered to life and an image of the Black Pearl's face appeared.

"Mr. Crane?"

"What is it?"

"I want to see you in my office."

"I'm busy."

"Then get un-busy," she said furiously.

"What's the problem?"

"The problem is *you*, and if you're not here in ten minutes' time, I am personally going to throw you off the *Comet*." She broke the connection.

6.

The Black Pearl sat, back erect, knees pressed tensely together, on one of the couches in her office.

Her hair was done in a number of small braids, each tipped at the end with a gold teardrop. A gold band, possessing large rubies and turquoises placed at regular intervals, circled her head like a crown. About her neck and shoulders she wore a flat gold collar composed of numerous six-inch strips of gold and tipped by rubies. Her breasts and midriff were bare, while her skirt was made of perhaps twenty metal strips, also gold. Her feet were wrapped in golden sandals, and she wore a golden band on her left arm.

The Dragon Lady, wearing a dark blue robe, sat opposite her on the facing sofa, nervously smoking a Denebian cigarette.

"He'll be here in just another minute or two," she said at last.

"I know," said the Black Pearl.

"Are you sure you don't want to change your clothes?"

"I'm a businesswoman. These are my business clothes."

"But—"

"One way or another we're going to get things straightened out around here," said the Black Pearl. "Crane wouldn't hesitate to use every advantage he could think of if he had called this meeting, so why should I?"

The Dragon Lady shrugged. "Have it your own way. To tell you the truth, I don't even know why I'm here, unless it's to play the role of the referee."

"You're here because this concerns the well-being of the *Comet*."

"Well, I just wish I were anywhere else. I see a confrontation coming up, and I don't want to get involved in it. After all, I have to work with both of you."

"There won't be any confrontation unless he wants one," said the Black Pearl.

"Of course there will," said the Security Chief. "You know he's attracted to you, and yet look at the way you're dressed. He may be many things, good and bad, but he's not stupid. He'll know why you're wearing this outfit, and he'll feel resentful and antagonistic."

"I'll settle for uncomfortable."

"I think we'll *all* be uncomfortable before this thing is over. I'd much rather go look at your Night Crystals."

"You can do the next best thing," said the Black Pearl. "Move over to the bar and sit on one of the stools. That way you'll be out of the line of verbal fire."

"Gladly," replied the Dragon Lady, crossing the

room. "And the fact that he'll now have to sit on the couch across from you wouldn't have anything to do with your altruism, would it?"

The Black Pearl offered her a predatory smile. "Perhaps just a little."

They sat in silence for another minute, and then the security system beeped twice.

"He's here," announced the Dragon Lady.

"I know."

"Well?"

"Let him knock."

A moment later Crane knocked on the door and the Black Pearl ordered it to open.

The detective stepped into the room, stared at the Black Pearl for a moment, then turned and nodded a greeting to the Dragon Lady.

"Cleopatra?" he asked, turning back to the madam. "Or one of the Roman goddesses?"

"Cleopatra," replied the Black Pearl, stretching her arms along the top of the sofa.

"I always thought she was bitten by an asp. Now I get the distinct impression that she died of a chest cold."

"Sit down, Mr. Crane," said the Black Pearl.

He looked around the room, saw that the chairs were too far away, shrugged, and walked over to the couch.

"What did you want to see me about?" he said, trying unsuccessfully to focus his attention solely on her face.

"I'll get right to the point," she said, crossing her legs and leaning back on the sofa. "I thought we were supposed to be working in concert."

"We are," he assured her.

"Then what's the idea of creating a Priority File?"

"So *that's* what this is all about," he replied.

"That's just a hint of what this is all about. This is *my* ship, and nobody—not you, not anybody—keeps secrets from me on my ship."

"I wasn't keeping them from *you*."

"From who, then?"

"From everybody."

"Why?"

"Because there are certain matters that, in my professional judgment, should remain confidential."

"Your professional judgment doesn't count for anything on the *Comet*—and see if you can concentrate on my face when I'm talking to you."

"I'm getting just a little tired of your telling me what I should and shouldn't do!" replied Crane heatedly. "I'll say what I want and look where I want. My job is catching killers. Yours is laying on your back and staring at the ceiling. What gives you the right to order me around?"

"I run the *Comet*—that's what gives me the right."

"Yeah? Well, it's about time you remembered who owns it and who's the goddamned hired help!" continued Crane. "The *owners* are paying me to do a job here, and I won't have you or anyone else telling me how to do it." He paused, then continued speaking in a more reasonable tone of voice. "Look. There's no way in hell you can keep this thing hushed up forever. My function is to clean this mess up before it becomes public, and I can't do it if you try to tie my hands. Now, do you want this killer caught before the shit hits the fan, or don't you?"

They were interrupted as the tabletop computer

produced a holographic image of one of the women at the reception desk.

"Yes?" said the Black Pearl distractedly.

"Mrs. Weiboldt has just left for the fantasy room."

"Tell her I'll be a few minutes late," replied the Black Pearl irritably, breaking the connection.

Crane waited until he had her full attention once again. "Just out of curiosity," he said, "why the hell were you spying on me in the first place?"

"I wasn't."

"Then how did you know I set up a Priority File?"

"That was *my* doing, Mr. Crane," interrupted the Dragon Lady from her seat by the bar.

Crane turned to her. "I almost forgot you were here," he commented.

"I can't imagine why," she replied dryly, looking meaningfully at the Black Pearl. "Anyway, the computer is programmed to let me know whenever a Priority File is initiated, and my standing orders are to inform my superiors. The only two superiors I have on board are you and the Black Pearl, so I immediately told her what had happened." She smiled. "It seemed a little pointless to inform you of your own actions."

"You should have cleared it with me first," said Crane.

"She followed her instructions to the letter," said the Black Pearl. "And I, for one, intend to enter a commendation on her record for her prompt action."

"Oh, it'll go on her record, all right," promised Crane. "I guarantee it."

"May I respectfully suggest that my record isn't the issue here?" said the Dragon Lady.

"You're absolutely right," agreed the Black Pearl.

"It's Mr. Crane and his continued refusal to treat us as anything other than unreliable coolie labor."

The Security Chief shook her head. "If you'll forgive my saying so," she replied patiently, "it's *both* of you."

"I don't suppose you'd care to justify that statement?" said the Black Pearl.

"For some reason, Mr. Crane has so little trust and confidence in you and me that he found it necessary to hide what he's doing from us; and, conversely, for some reason, you have so little trust and confidence in Mr. Crane that you feel it incumbent upon you to force him to open that Priority File. I think you're both so busy sparring with each other that you've forgotten who the real enemy is."

"The real enemy," said the Black Pearl, "is anyone who endangers my ship in any way."

"And did using a Priority File damage the *Comet?*" asked the Dragon Lady mildly.

"I won't know until I've seen and heard it, will I?" said the Black Pearl. "But it's been my observation that Mr. Crane doesn't give a damn about the welfare of the ship or the happiness of its patrons. Just whose side are you on, anyway?"

"Since I'm the one who has to work with both of you, I'm on the side of accommodation," replied the Dragon Lady. "Mr. Crane," she continued, turning to the detective, "can you tell us, if not explicitly, at least in a broad general manner, exactly what is in that Priority File?"

"Of course I can."

"Will you?"

"Well, now, that's another question," he said. "If I

tell the two of you as much as I feel you should know, will you get off my back?"

"That depends on what you tell us," said the Black Pearl.

Crane shook his head. "You've got two choices: you can agree to my terms and accept what I'm willing to tell you, or you can refuse to agree, in which case I won't tell you a damned thing. There's no third way."

"I don't like ultimatums," said the Black Pearl.

"Then you shouldn't force me to deliver them."

She stared at him coldly. "All right," she said at last. "It's a deal."

He turned to the Dragon Lady. "Do you agree too?"

"I was never going to question you in the first place," she replied. "I merely followed a given procedure."

"All right," he said. "Cupid, do you know who this is?"

YOU ARE ANDREW JACKSON CRANE.

"Right. Everything that gets said in this room goes into my Priority File we created until I tell you to close it."

WORKING . . . READY.

Crane turned from the computer, found himself staring at the Black Pearl's bare breasts, and forced himself to look across the room at the Security Chief.

"I know why Infante was killed," he announced at last.

"To scare someone—or so you said," commented the Dragon Lady.

"But now I know *who* the murder was meant to scare," replied Crane. "And I think I know what the murderer was trying to scare him into doing. I didn't put it into a Priority File to keep it from you; I put it there because if either the killer or the man he was trying to frighten found out what I knew, we'd never get to the bottom of this thing."

"And now you can?" asked the Black Pearl.

He nodded confidently. "I can deliver the killer to you by tomorrow morning."

"Why tomorrow?" demanded the Black Pearl. "Why don't you make an arrest right now?"

"I intend to," he said.

"Then that's that," said the madam. "What the hell was the big secret?"

"I think I know," interjected the Dragon Lady softly.

"Well?" insisted the Black Pearl.

The Dragon Lady smiled at Crane. "The man you're going to arrest isn't the killer, is he?"

Crane returned her smile. "You're a pretty sharp old lady," he said.

"I'll forgive you the 'old lady', and thank you for the rest."

"Will someone tell me what's going on here?" said the Black Pearl.

"I don't know who the killer is," said Crane. "He's covered his tracks pretty well."

The Black Pearl frowned. "I thought you knew all about how and why he killed Infante."

"Not *those* tracks. What he did aboard the *Comet* is very easy to recreate," replied Crane. "It's his tracks from New Sumatra *to* the *Comet* that are the problem."

"New Sumatra?" repeated the madam. "What's *that* got to do with anything?"

"More than you suppose," said Crane. "The man the killer was trying to scare was on New Sumatra during the Bello Affair."

"The Bello Affair? I remember reading about it. Wasn't Bello the one they called the Bloody Butcher?"

Crane nodded. "Yes."

"And Infante was there at the same time?"

"No. He showed up a couple of years later."

"Then what's the tie-in?"

"They were both on Deluros VIII at the same time."

The Black Pearl smiled condescendingly. "There are nine billion people on Deluros. Are you trying to tell me that Edward Infante was the only one who'd ever been to New Sumatra?"

"No," said Crane. "But he's the only one who had been to New Sumatra and wound up getting killed aboard the *Comet*. He made trips from Deluros to the *Comet* on a regular basis."

"So do thousands of other men and women," she pointed out.

"True," agreed Crane. "But he didn't start coming up here until after you'd hired the man the killer was trying to scare. He must have been a contact—some kind of go-between."

"Between who and who?"

"Between the man I'm going to arrest, and whatever New Sumatran organization has set up shop on Deluros VIII."

"You're absolutely sure of this?" asked the Black Pearl.

"I am."

"What does Cupid say?"

"I see you're calling him by my name," he noted smugly.

"What does he say?"

"He doesn't say I'm wrong."

"Does he say you're right?"

"It's not that simple," said Crane. "Cupid is capable of analyzing trillions upon trillions of bits of information, which means he can not only see the likeliest possibility, but *every* possibility, no matter how remote. He won't say I'm right until he has so much information—by which I mean proof—that only one possibility remains."

She frowned. "Then we have to rely upon your expertise."

"I told you once before: I'm the best there is."

"And I believe I commented upon your modesty once before," she replied. She stared at him for a moment. "All right, Mr. Crane: you have studiously avoided mentioning the name of the man you intend to arrest. Why?"

"I don't know what either of your relationships are to him. I have to have your word that you won't try to hinder me once I tell you who it is."

"You have my promise," said the Dragon Lady.

"How much danger will you be putting him in?" asked the Black Pearl.

"I don't know," replied Crane honestly.

"All right," she said, after a moment's consideration.

"It's Esteban Morales," said Crane.

"Esteban?" said the Black Pearl, surprised. "I just made a holo for him last week."

"A holo?" repeated Crane, suddenly aware of her costume once again.

"A holographic entertainment," she explained.

"You mean a pornographic entertainment."

"If you wish," she said, aware of his gaze and his

ill-concealed discomfort. "I made it with Sugar Daddy and Totem Pole." She paused. "It was a rather good one, if I say so myself."

"I'm sure you'd be the best judge of that," he replied.

"You can see it if you'd like," she said with a catlike grin. "Tell Cupid to shift to video mode and turn to Channel 37Q."

"I'll keep it in mind."

"Who knows?" she added with a shrug. "You might learn something."

"Excuse me," interrupted the Dragon Lady. "But what exactly do you propose to accomplish by arresting Morales?"

Crane turned to the Security Chief. "One of two things," he replied. "I know that the killer was trying to frighten Morales, but I don't know if he was trying to scare him into *doing* something or *not* doing it. Now, if he wanted Morales to do something badly enough to kill Infante, then he's going to have to try to make contact with Morales before we ship him off to Deluros for his mythical trial."

"But if he was trying to get Morales to stop, won't this do his job for him?" asked the Dragon Lady.

"Yes—but, again, if it was important enough to precipitate a murder, then I can probably make a trade with Morales: his freedom to keep doing whatever it was, in exchange for the killer's identity."

"What if neither happens?" asked the Black Pearl. "What if the killer doesn't try to make contact and Morales won't deal?"

"One or the other has got to happen," said Crane with certainty.

"You could wind up looking pretty silly if you're wrong," said the Black Pearl.

"Sillier than you think," replied Crane. "I want the media up here."

"What are you talking about?" demanded the Black Pearl.

"I want this arrest to be big and noisy," he answered. "I don't want to take a chance on the killer missing it." He paused. "We'll let them stick around and hand them the real killer tomorrow morning. I figure it'll take them about six hours to get up here, so I'll make the arrest about midnight and—"

"Not a chance!" said the Black Pearl firmly. "We're not having the media up here, and that's absolutely non-negotiable."

"It'll work much better with them," said Crane.

"Mr. Crane, it's bad enough that we've had a murder on the *Comet*. I cannot and will not allow you to make public the fact that the richest and most influential men and women in the Republic have shared an enclosed environment for almost five days with a killer whose identity is still unknown to you."

"Do you want him captured or not?"

She stared straight into his eyes. "If you can't catch him without making a public spectacle out of it, then I don't want him captured." She paused. "Earlier we were just jockeying for position, but this is in earnest. The *Velvet Comet* is like any other resort: it lives or dies with its reputation. And I will not allow it to have the reputation of being a haven for killers"—she paused—"or for publicity-seeking detectives, either."

"I resent that!" he snapped.

"Resent it all you like," she replied. "But don't waste your breath denying it."

The Dragon Lady seemed about to say something, then thought better of it and remained silent.

"You don't know what you're talking about," said Crane.

"I think we *both* know," replied the Black Pearl. "I've seen your dossier, I know how rapidly you've advanced and how ambitious you are. Understanding people is my business, Mr. Crane, contrary to what you may think. We don't need the media up here. The ship has a public address system, and Cupid can send messages to any member of the crew and any room in the ship. If you want the media up here, it's so they can disseminate holographs and stories about how the fearless young detective single-handedly captured yet another vicious killer. Except that the end result of your actions will be to cost the *Comet* millions of credits and untold confidence. I can't allow it."

"You're wrong," he said without much sincerity. "But what the hell—let it be. No publicity."

"When and where will you make the arrest?" asked the Dragon Lady.

"Probably as soon as I leave here," replied Crane. "We'll have Cupid flash it on every screen in the place at ten-minute intervals."

"You haven't been listening to a word I've said," interjected the Black Pearl. "I don't want the patrons to know there was a murder aboard the *Comet*."

"Just how long do you think you can keep this thing quiet?" said Crane. "Sooner or later the killer is going to stand trial in a public court of law."

"I'll worry about that when the time comes," she

replied. "Right now I'll just settle for later rather than sooner."

"They'll be just as mad at you when they find out you've been hiding a murder from them," he said.

"I have a suggestion that may solve that problem," said the Dragon Lady, walking over to stand next to the detective's couch.

"Go ahead," said Crane.

"What if we were to announce that two crew members got into a fight this morning and one of them killed the other? If we say it happened in the Home, that would hardly be a cause for concern among the patrons."

"Good," said Crane, nodding his head. "I think it will work."

"How do we let the killer know what's going on?" asked the Black Pearl.

"We announce that the name of the dead crew member is Edward Infante," replied Crane. "The killer will be smart enough to figure out that we're lying so that the patrons won't be frightened. He'll know it's the same Infante."

"And if one of the patrons knew Infante?"

"I don't think it's very likely," said Crane. "But if anyone knew him, the chances are that they knew why he was killed. I think they'll keep their mouths shut."

"All right," said the Black Pearl. "I can agree to that."

"Then it's settled?" asked the Dragon Lady.

"Almost," said Crane. "According to Cupid, Infante slept with seven different prostitutes during his various trips here. Is it possible to confine them to their rooms and keep them incommunicado for the next 24 hours?"

"Because they knew Infante was a patron instead of a crew member, you mean?" asked the Black Pearl.

"Right."

She shook her head. "Where would you stop? Every receptionist knows his name; he had a line of credit at the casino, which means the pit boss and some of the accountants knew him; he couldn't have eaten in the restaurants without reservations, which means most of the waiters know his name: he—"

"I get the picture," interrupted Crane. He lowered his head in thought for a minute, then looked up. "All right. What we'll do is this: Cupid will announce that there is an important general message waiting on the computer for every employee of the *Comet*. When they check it out, he'll tell them that for the security of the ship—and more to the point, for the security of their jobs—they must not contradict any information concerning Infante during the next 24 hours. Each of them will have to acknowledge the message by signing their personal code, and by 1800 hours we'll disseminate it to the stragglers." He paused. "Can they be trusted to do what they're told? The patrons are probably going to ask about it when we announce that Morales was arrested for killing Infante."

"If we word it so that they know, in no uncertain terms, that they'll be terminated for contradicting the announcement, I think they'll keep quiet," said the Black Pearl.

"And if one of them *does* contradict it," added the Dragon Lady, "at least we'll have a likely suspect."

"Well," said Crane, "I guess that's everything. Cupid?"

YES?

"Close the Priority File again."

CLOSED.

"Did anyone try to monitor us while the file was open?"

NO . . . URGENT MESSAGE COMING IN.

A woman's face, the same one that had appeared earlier, materialized.

"I hate to bother you again," she said, "but Mrs. Weiboldt's just about to throw a tantrum. She only has the room for another 75 minutes."

"Give her a one-hour extension," said the Black Pearl.

"It's booked again 20 minutes after she's through with it," replied the woman.

"Shit!" muttered the Black Pearl. "All right. Tell her I'm on my way." She broke the connection and walked to the door. "I've got to leave," she said to them. "I have no objection to the plan you've outlined, but I insist on being informed if you decide to change it in any way."

"Fair enough," agreed Crane. Then he added, with just a touch of sardonicism, "Have fun."

"I intend to," she replied, walking out into the corridor.

"What was that all about?" asked Crane, as the door slid shut behind her.

"Mrs. Weiboldt is a 73-year-old lady who's worth about seven billion credits," said the Dragon Lady. "I think her family made their money in mining, out in the Altair region. At any rate, she is what one might call a voyeur with delusions of literacy."

"What does *that* mean?"

"It means that she comes up here once every two

or three months, rents a fantasy room, hires a cast of 15 or 20 of us, and turns the script to her latest epic over to the Black Pearl, who does the casting. Today the Black Pearl is playing Cleopatra to Totem Pole's Mark Antony." She paused. "It cost us almost two million credits to adapt the Roman Room for this."

"Adapt it?" queried Crane.

"You haven't seen our fantasy rooms yet, have you?" she replied. "We have 36 of them, each rather large—and with a few carefully-selected props and a batch of holographic projectors and scents and sound effects, we turn them into tropical paradises, mountaintop ski lodges, domed underwater bedrooms, and the like. Not always realistic, mind you—after all, most medieval throne rooms were cold and dirty and generally unappetizing—but totally believable to the senses, and the imagination takes care of the rest. Most of the rooms are what you might call set pieces; we can change them, like we're doing for Mrs. Weiboldt, but it costs a lot of money. Fortunately, she has a lot of money to spend. I think the barge alone will run her half a million credits."

"Does she just pull up a chair and watch, or does she have to use the holographic screen in her room?"

The Dragon Lady looked amused. "Neither. She writes herself into the script. Today she's Cleopatra's nurse."

"And she just stands around telling everybody what to do?"

"We cater to some rather unique tastes," admitted the Security Chief.

"And the Black Pearl has to cater to them personally?" he said, frowning.

"No. She's the madam. She doesn't have to do anything she doesn't want to do."

He shook his head. "I don't understand her."

"I think it may be mutual," replied the Dragon Lady.

"Probably," he admitted. He stood up and walked restlessly around the office, finally stopping in front of the holographs of the previous madams.

"Were they *all* like her?" he asked.

"I only knew eight of them personally," answered the Dragon Lady. "The only thing they had in common was a single-minded devotion to the *Comet*." She smiled. "One doesn't become the madam of the *Velvet Comet* by emulating the previous madam, Mr. Crane, but rather by applying one's ambition and competence in unique ways. Of course, I can't speak for the five who went before me, but the ones I've known have all been remarkable women."

"You have male prostitutes," he noted. "How come you've never had a male madam?"

"We have a highly-charged sexual atmosphere up here," she explained. "Men tend to become too aggressive when put under pressure, and the madam's job is the most pressure-laden I know of."

"That sounds like an unreasonable sexual prejudice," remarked Crane.

"Prejudice, yes; unreasonable, no. Other establishments have used male madams, and a well-run business learns at least as much from its competitors' errors as from its own."

He shrugged. "Then I was wrong about the missing picture. I thought it might be of a man."

"I beg your pardon?"

"When I mentioned that there were eleven previous madams, the Black Pearl corrected me and said that there had been twelve, but that Vainmill refused to hang one of the holographs."

"Vainmill has an interesting notion of morality," commented the Dragon Lady dryly. "The missing holograph is of a woman named Suma, who became the madam when she was nineteen, and was fired two months later for her involvement in the death of her predecessor."

"What makes that kind of morality interesting?" asked Crane.

"She's the only former madam that Vainmill still does business with."

"What kind of business?"

"She runs a school of sorts on Delvania III," said the Dragon Lady. "It's where the *Comet's* recruits get their training."

"A school for prostitutes?" he said dubiously. "What the hell is there to learn?"

"More than you imagine," she replied. "Not all of our prostitutes come from Delvania, but the ones who do are exquisitely gifted and masterfully trained. That much I'll grant her."

"If they've got nothing but potential prostitutes there, who do they practice on?"

"Each other, and an occasional guest of the management."

"Were *you* trained there?"

She shook her head. "It wasn't that well established when I was starting out."

"How old is this Suma, anyway?"

"In her mid-50s, I should imagine. I've seen a few holographs of her, and I must confess that she was the most beautiful of our madams, which is no small accomplishment."

He took a last look at the eleven striking women, then stretched once and turned to the Dragon Lady.

"I think it's about time we got to work," he said. "Give me about ten minutes to program Cupid with the message, and another hour to track Morales down and arrest him, and then you can make your announcement."

"All right," she replied. "I think I'll do it from my office. I can coordinate things better from there."

"Where did you plan on keeping Morales?" he asked her.

"We have a detention cell in the Security area."

He shook his head. "I want him confined to his own quarters. Just put him there, change the coding on the lock so he can't get out, and don't post a guard."

"So you really think the killer will try to make contact with him?"

"I don't know," lied Crane. "But if he does, let's not make it too difficult for him. I assume you have cameras in the hall?"

"Of course."

"Make sure they're working."

"I'll check them out personally."

"Good," said Crane getting to his feet. "Now let's go to work."

And let's hope, he added mentally as he stepped aside and allowed her to pass through the doorway ahead of him, that you don't figure out what's *really* going to happen and wind up costing me my life.

7.

Crane arrested a very surprised Morales at 1200 hours, ship's time, waited long enough to make sure that Cupid was disseminating the information, and then went to bed. He awoke at 2100 hours, feeling much refreshed, quickly shaved and showered, replaced his gray businessman's suit with a metallic black one, and took the elevator up to the main level of the Resort.

He discovered that the Cosmic Room was booked solid through midnight, found a different restaurant that managed to accommodate him without a reservation, and spent the next hour dining on sautéed meats and flaming soufflés.

Finally, his hunger sated, he paid his first visit to the casino. It was a huge and opulent room, fully 200 feet long and 150 wide. Enormous crystal chandeliers provided more than ample illumination, and a number of waiters and waitresses were moving unobtrusively through the room, dispensing free drinks to anyone who was playing at the gaming tables.

He had been to casinos on Deluros and a handful of other worlds, and had usually been disappointed in them. Romantic fictions and cinemas had always portrayed them as the playgrounds for the very rich, whereas his experience was that the typical casino gambler had no more knowledge of taste or culture than he had of odds.

The *Velvet Comet's* casino was more in line with what he had anticipated before he had actually gone out into the adult world. The noise was subdued, the faces of the participants reflected a sense of enjoyment rather than tension or frightened expectation, the dress mode was elegant, the behavior sedate. As he wandered in among the tables, he became aware of a string quartet performing in a far corner of the room. Holographs gave the illusion of a number of balconies overlooking a clear blue sea at twilight.

The tables were grouped by games—roulette, craps, baccarat, chemin de fer, blackjack, and a smattering of contests that were totally alien in origin—and there was a row of terminals lined up near one of the bars where contestants could match wits with Cupid in a variety of games ranging from chess to trivia. One section of the room had been turned over to a bookmaking parlour, where men and women sat in comfortable lounge chairs, made their selections on computer terminals, and then watched live holographs of various sporting contests that were transmitted up from Deluros VIII.

There was a stage near the center of the casino, right between the baccarat and roulette tables, on which a procession of nude and nearly-nude women executed graceful and intricate dances to the music of the quartet. Crane watched them for a few minutes, marveling at the sensual fluidity of their movements, and finding them far more erotic than the blatant entertainments he had seen elsewhere in his travels. He had a premonition that if he actually watched one of the Black Pearl's video performances he would find it more artistic than pornographic.

He spent the next hour wandering through the casino, stopping every now and then to watch the action at one of the tables. When he felt he had made himself visible enough, he took his leave and walked over to the nightclub.

He was ushered to a table near the stage, ordered a cup of coffee, and settled back to watch the show.

Pagliacci, wearing his usual clown's make-up, was on stage, rattling off a string of jokes that were older than the *Comet*. Nobody in the audience seemed to mind, however, and he received a fair share of amused laughter and an occasional guffaw.

"Actually, I've finally got the hang of it," the comedian was saying. "I drink my Scotch straight"—he paused—"and my gin horizontal." He waited for the scattered chuckles to subside. "To tell you the truth, I only drink to steady my nerves. Sometimes they get so steady I can't move."

Suddenly his eyes fell on Crane.

"Let's have a round of applause for Andrew Jackson Crane, the fearless detective who just arrested the crewman responsible for a rather unpleasant incident down at the other end of the *Comet*."

There was a round of polite applause, and Crane, startled, half-rose and nodded his head.

"You'll notice that my friend Detective Crane is sipping a cup of coffee. Coming here for coffee is like going to your suite for a nap." Scattered laughter.

"Truth to tell, Mr. Crane never drinks anything stronger than pop—and Pop drinks anything."

Pagliacci kept up his ancient and inoffensive patter for another five minutes, while Crane finished his coffee and ordered a second cup.

"It's time for my act to close, Mr. Crane," Pagliacci announced, "and you still haven't cracked a smile."

"Maybe I'm in a bad mood," said Crane.

"I promised Mr. Crane that I wouldn't get off the stage until I got a laugh out of him," the comedian announced to the audience. "So unless one of you lovely ladies would like to walk over and tickle him, you're going to have to put up with a few more jokes."

Polite if unenthusiastic applause followed.

"All right," said Pagliacci grimly. "Moses comes down from the mountain and says, 'I've got some good news and some bad news. The good news is that I've talked Him down to ten . . . and the bad news is that adultery is still on the list.'"

Crane stared at him expressionlessly.

Pagliacci cleared his throat nervously. "Okay," he said. "Jesus is wandering through Heaven, looking for his father, when finally, after days of fruitless searching, he sees a bearded old patriarch sitting on a bench. He suddenly realizes that he's exhausted, so he goes and sits down on the bench too. They get to talking, and Jesus tells the old man that he's been searching for his father.

" 'That's odd,' says the old man. 'I've been searching for my son.'

" 'My father was a carpenter,' says Jesus.

" '*I* was a carpenter,' replies the old man.

"Suddenly Jesus is interested.

" 'My father's name was Joseph,' he says.

" 'Well, in your language, I suppose *my* name would be Joseph,' says the old man.

" 'The man I'm looking for wasn't actually my father, though he raised me from the day I was born,' says Jesus.

" 'It's funny you should say that,' answers the old man. 'Because I wasn't really my son's father, though I acted in that capacity from the instant he first drew breath.'

"Jesus and the old man stare long and hard at each other.

" 'Father?' says Jesus.

"A tear comes to the old man's eye.

" '*Pinnochio?*' "

Two men and a woman almost fell off their chairs, but there was absolutely no reaction from the remainder of the audience.

"Who the hell is Pinnochio?" asked Crane.

"Damn it!" said Pagliacci irritably. "If you knew anything about your race's myths and folklore, you'd be rolling around on the floor laughing your head off. You've got to bring a little something to the performance; I can't supply it all."

"They say that humor's a very subjective thing," replied Crane calmly.

"Well, they're wrong. Some things are funny by any criteria." The comedian looked grimly determined. "I'll try one more."

Crane sensed the restlessness of the audience, and made up his mind to laugh no matter how unfunny the joke was. It turned out to be a five-minute story that led up to a truly horrible pun, and when it was done and he had forced himself to chuckle, Pagliacci finally took his bows and turned the stage over to the singer.

"Mind if I join you?" asked the comedian, approaching Crane's table.

"Be my guest," replied Crane. "Or, to be more precise, be Vainmill's guest."

"Thanks," said Pagliacci, pulling up a chair. He stared intently at the detective for a moment. "You didn't really think it was funny, did you?"

"I laughed, didn't I?" responded Crane.

"Insincerely."

"Well, you can't have everything."

"No," admitted the comedian. "But you can *want* everything."

Crane made no reply, and Pagliacci signalled to a waiter and ordered a drink.

"Care for one?" he asked. "My treat."

"No, thanks," said Crane. "I don't drink."

"I know," grinned Pagliacci. "That's why I offered."

"Maybe we should be quiet for awhile," suggested Crane. "We seem to be bothering the singer."

"Tough," said Pagliacci. "People talk during *my* act all the time. It's an occupational hazard, like people lying to a detective."

"Why would anyone want to lie to me?"

"People are afraid of what detectives might discover about their pasts, just as they're afraid of what doctors might discover about their bodies."

"I take it that you're not one of them."

"I've got nothing to hide." The comedian smiled. "Which isn't to say that I don't owe you a couple of whoppers."

"I don't think I follow you," replied Crane.

"You told me that this Infante was an embezzler.

Now suddenly I find out that he's a murder victim. You lied to me."

"Don't take it personally," said Crane. "I lied to everyone."

"Why?"

"You ought to be grateful to me," replied the detective. "If you're this bad when you're relaxed, think of how unfunny you'd be if you thought there was a killer in the audience."

The comedian seemed about to make an angry retort, then shrugged. "What the hell—you're right. I died up there tonight. That's what comes of telling the same jokes every week."

"They're pretty awful," commented Crane.

"Are you this polite to everyone?" asked Pagliacci. "Or is there something about me personally that brings out the best in you?"

"I thought you didn't want me to lie to you," said Crane.

"What I wanted was to make you laugh," replied the comedian. Suddenly his face lit up with renewed enthusiasm. "Tell you what: I've got a detective routine that's an absolute knockout. As soon as this idiot is through murdering her obligatos, I'll perform it for you right here at the table."

"Why are you so bound and determined to amuse me?" asked Crane with a touch of irritation.

"Because you represent a challenge."

"Some other time," said Crane, rising to his feet.

"Need a little company?" offered the comedian. "I'm not due on stage again for almost three hours."

"Suit yourself."

"Fine. Where are you going?"

"The casino."

Pagliacci shook his head. "I'd better not," he said. "I've already lost too much money there." He smiled. "No will power." He leaned back on his chair. "See you around."

"I doubt it," said Crane. "I'm taking Morales back to Deluros tomorrow morning."

"Then you'll always be the one that got away," said Pagliacci. "If you'll leave your address at the reception desk, maybe I'll mail you a tape of that routine."

"Don't do it right away," replied Crane. "Give me something to live for."

He turned and walked out of the nightclub.

He made brief appearances in the other three clubs, then wandered back to the casino, where he spent another half hour being visible. Finally he checked the time and began wending his way to the reception foyer.

Once there he entered a private communications booth and put through a call to the Dragon Lady. Her image appeared before him a moment later, and from her surroundings it was obvious that she was very near Morales' room.

"How's it going?" he asked.

"Everything's quiet so far," she replied.

"Okay," he said. "I think it's time to entice our man out into the open. He's only got about eight hours left before I'm supposed to leave with Morales, and we don't want to scare him so much that he doesn't make an attempt."

"What do you want me to do?" asked the Dragon Lady.

"Put every member of your staff that you can spare in the Resort's public rooms, and make them as visible as possible. We don't want our killer thinking that they're all waiting for him in Morales' room. Then pull everyone who's left off the level Morales is on, but position them so they can get there in a hurry."

"That might look too obvious," she said. "What if I station one man by the door, but with strict instructions to look something less than alert?"

"Good idea," agreed Crane. He tried to hide his tension as he issued the only order that mattered. "I also want you to shut down the security system at the Resort's tramway entrance for the next two hours."

"Why?" asked the Dragon Lady. "Since he's a member of the crew, he's cleared for it anyway."

"I had Cupid rig it to register weapons," lied Crane. "I don't want alarms going off all the hell over and scaring him away if he happens to be carrying a pistol."

"It seems to me that he's more likely to just have a knife—or if he *does* have a more formidable weapon, it's probably hidden in his room. Besides, we don't know for a fact that he isn't in the Mall or the Home right now."

"If he's not in the Resort, then there's no harm done," said Crane tersely. "If he is, let's make it as easy as possible for him to get where he wants to go."

She sighed. "You're the boss."

"I'll check in with you in a couple of hours."

"Where can I reach you if something happens in the meantime?"

"Oh, I'll be around. Just have Cupid page me."

He broke the connection, spent the next half hour forcing himself to read stock quotations off a large monitor in the reception foyer, then walked over to the escalator and descended to the tramway level.

He walked up to the computer's retina scanner, breathed a sigh of relief when it didn't respond to him, then opened the gate that led to the platform.

The tramcar was nowhere to be seen, and he quickly jumped down into the tunnel and began walking rapidly, slowing his pace only when he felt he was far enough from the platform so that no one could see him. He ducked into a maintenance port as the tramcar passed by, remained there until it picked up a handful of passengers from the Resort and headed back toward the Home, and then resumed walking.

Finally he reached the port where Infante's body had been found, wedged himself into it, sat down, and waited.

Ten minutes passed, then twenty, and finally half an hour. He was just on the point of admitting to himself that he had guessed wrong when he heard footsteps approaching. He waited until they were quite close, then rose to his feet and stepped out into the tunnel.

"Hi, Andy," said Pagliacci with a friendly smile. He carried a bottle of chilled champagne in one hand, and two crystal glasses in the other. "I think it's time that you and I had a little chat."

"Well, I'll be damned!" said Crane. "So it's *you*!"

"What are you acting so surprised about?" asked Pagliacci easily. "You sure as hell look like you were expecting company."

"I knew someone would be along," replied Crane. "I just didn't know who."

"Some detective!" snorted Pagliacci with a chuckle. "I don't ever want to hear you criticize my comedy routines again." Crane pulled a small handgun out of his pocket and trained it on the comedian.

"Careful how you point that thing, Andy," said Pagliacci. "I'd hate to see you miss me and hit this beautiful bottle."

"How long has Stanley Dombroski been dead?" asked Crane suddenly.

"Oh, a long time," replied Pagliacci. "Ten or twelve years now. I've been reciting his idiotic jokes for so long that I'm really getting rather good at it, your criticisms notwithstanding."

"And who are you?"

"I'm the guy who wants to talk to you without being overheard." He paused. "You chose a nice place. I've always had a fondness for returning to the scene of the crime."

"Talk all you want," said Crane. "But when you're through, I'm going to arrest you for the murder of Edward Infante."

Pagliacci shook his head and smiled confidently. "When I'm through, what you're going to do is *thank* me."

"You think so?"

"I *know* so. This may seem a little difficult for you to believe, but before the night is over you and I are going to be partners."

"You haven't done your homework," remarked Crane dryly. "I'm every bit as ambitious and incorruptible as I'm supposed to be."

"I certainly hope so," replied Pagliacci. "I'm counting on it."

He popped open the champagne and filled the two glasses.

8.

"There's another service port just across the tunnel," said Pagliacci, jerking his head in its direction. "Do you mind if I sit there? The tram could come by any minute, and I get just a little nervous standing out here."

"Be my guest," replied Crane, keeping his weapon trained on the comedian.

"Thanks. And, since you're not a drinker, I hope you won't mind if I take both glasses with me."

"Not at all."

Pagliacci walked some fifteen feet to the port, stepped into it, and carefully lowered himself to the ground. "Good stuff," he remarked as he took a sip from one of the glasses after placing the other on the floor. "You don't know what you're missing." He paused. "Were you really going to take Morales to Deluros if I hadn't approached you?"

Crane shrugged. "It never occurred to me that someone wouldn't try to stop me. I should have figured out that you'd be the one."

"Don't go blaming yourself for not knowing. I was pretty careful: you didn't have much to go on."

"I had one thing," contradicted Crane. "Whoever killed Infante couldn't wait five weeks until his next visit—and your contract is up in three more weeks."

"True," agreed Pagliacci thoughtfully. "I probably should have killed him during his last visit. I just kept hoping that I wouldn't have to."

"Is this as big as I think it is?" asked Crane suddenly.

"Probably," said Pagliacci. "But you tell me what you think, and I'll tell you if you're right."

"You killed Infante to frighten Morales."

"Let's say that I did it to convince him of the urgency of the situation."

"He doesn't have anything you want, or you'd have taken it from him," continued Crane. "That was a very professional piece of work you did on Infante."

"He has *one* thing," contradicted Pagliacci. "But he'd have died before he gave it to me."

"Whatever he has, it's inside his head," said the detective. He waited for a reaction, but the comedian offered none. "He's either doing something that you want stopped, or not doing something that you want started."

"So far, so good."

"I knew that after I'd been here two hours," said Crane disdainfully. "The trick was figuring out what it was you wanted him to do, and why."

Pagliacci drained his glass, placed it down, and picked up the other one. "And did you figure it out?"

"I've got most of the pieces," replied the detective. "Maybe you can help me put them together."

The tramcar suddenly whizzed by.

"What do you think you've got?" asked the comedian, after it had passed.

"Well, for starters, I've got Morales and Infante."

"You've got Infante," corrected Pagliacci.

Crane shook his head. "I've got them both, or you wouldn't be here."

Pagliacci smiled. "I stand corrected."

"They'd been together only twice—on Deluros VIII and on the *Comet*. They had no business dealings, and there's no record of Infante ever meeting with Morales up here, though I suspect he must have."

"He did."

"I assume such meetings were his sole reason for coming here?"

"I think you could call that a fair assumption," agreed the comedian.

"They had one other thing in common," continued Crane. "They had both been to New Sumatra."

"But not at the same time," noted Pagliacci.

"That threw me for awhile," admitted the detective. "Until I checked to see if either of them had been there during the Bello Affair. Then I had it."

"And what did you have?" asked Pagliacci, amused.

"The connection. Morales was on New Sumatra during Bello's reign. Infante was there a few years later. They probably knew many of the same people. Then they were both on Deluros together. Then Morales came to work aboard the *Comet*, and immediately thereafter Infante became a regular patron."

"Are you suggesting that Infante was blackmailing Morales for something he had done on New Sumatra?"

"Not a chance. Either you or Morales might kill a blackmailer, but neither of you would then go out of your way to make sure the body was discovered while you were still on the ship."

"A telling point," commented Pagliacci. "You're as good as I thought you'd be."

"So, if the connection wasn't blackmail, then I have to assume they were working for a common cause, and that the cause has something to do with the Bello Affair."

"For example?"

"Well," said Crane, "now we get down to guesswork. I assume that some remnants of Bello's organization are headquartered on Deluros VIII. My guess is that Morales is some kind of contact man, and that Infante was a messenger. They couldn't converse by computer, since we'd have complete records of everything they said, so they had to meet in person. There's no place as secure as the tunnel, but I imagine Morales and Infante could have exchanged a few words in the casino or the reception foyer without being overheard."

"My own guess is that they passed written messages," interjected Pagliacci.

"Then I'm right?" asked Crane.

"Let's say that you're very warm."

"Then we come back to why you killed Infante," said Crane, "and I keep coming up with the conclusion that it was to make Morales *do* something. If you'd wanted him to *stop* doing it, you'd have killed *him* instead of murdering a patron and risking the kind of investigation you wound up with."

"Very good, Andy!" said Pagliacci. "I can see that you're going to make an excellent partner."

"Anyway," said Crane, ignoring his remark, "everything boils down to what you wanted Morales to do."

"That it does."

"And I keep coming up with the notion that, since he's a contact, you want him to get in touch with his superiors and tell them something."

"Absolutely right."

Crane stared at him. "I don't know a hell of a lot about New Sumatra, but I can't imagine that there's more than one man who makes this kind of risk worth taking."

Pagliacci smiled. "You've got it, Andy."

Crane nodded. "Bello's alive and hiding on Deluros VIII, isn't he?"

"A temporary yes to both questions," replied Pagliacci. "He's alive and he's on Deluros; neither condition is going to last a whole lot longer."

"How long has he been there?"

Pagliacci drained his second glass. "About five years."

"And how did you find out about it?"

"I'll be happy to tell you as soon as you put your weapon away," said Pagliacci. Crane hesitated. "Come on, Andy, you don't want *me*, not when I can give you the Bloody Butcher of New Sumatra. Hell, all I did was kill a man who was in the employ of a genocidal war criminal. It's not me you want—it's Bello. Think of what this can do for your career."

"I'm thinking."

"Then let me help you a little bit," said Pagliacci, and now he was no longer smiling. "If you take me in, you're going to find yourself giving testimony against a fucking hero. I'll admit to everything you say, and I'll still get off the hook."

"I assume you're willing to gamble your life on that?" said Crane dryly.

"On that, and on the fact that you're as incorruptible and ambitious as you think you are," answered Pagliacci. "If you don't agree to work with me, our conversation ends now. You'll never know how to draw Bello out of hiding, and better men than you have failed to find him on Deluros."

"There are no better men."

"*More* men, then," amended Pagliacci, momentarily surprised at the extent of the detective's ego. "But if you give me your word that you'll team up with me to capture Bello, I'll tell you what we have to do to get him up here."

"Up here? You mean to the *Comet*?"

Pagliacci nodded. "Have we got a deal?"

"I'm considering it."

"Well, consider it quickly. I'm due on stage in another hour."

Crane stared at him for a long minute.

"All right," he said at last, tucking his weapon away. "We're in business."

"Good. I knew you were a reasonable man."

"And now that we're partners, *you're* going to be a sober man. No more champagne."

"Oh, I'm pretty sober," said Pagliacci. He opened his left hand to reveal a tiny pistol. "I've had this trained on you the whole time, just in case we didn't strike a bargain."

"I know," said Crane calmly.

"The hell you did."

"I did," he repeated.

"Then why didn't you try to take it away from me?"

"Because I figured you were here to deal, not to kill me. Besides, that thing hasn't got much stopping power, and I guarantee you'd never get off a second shot." He snorted contemptuously. "Have you ever actually fired that toy?"

"More often than you might think," replied Pagliacci, replacing it in his pocket. "And I've never needed a second shot yet."

"If we're all through being macho, let's get down to facts. Who are you, and what's your interest in Quintus Bello? Are you a bounty hunter?"

"I'm Pagliacci."

"And the rest of it?"

"I'm no bounty hunter. I'm a citizen—expatriate, to be sure—of New Sumatra, and I've been hunting that bastard down for more than a decade."

"Alone?"

Pagliacci shook his head. "There's an organization."

Crane nodded thoughtfully. "There would almost have to be. If he's kept this well-hidden, one man alone could never hunt him down. How many people are behind you?"

"A lot."

"All New Sumatrans?"

"Some of us." Pagliacci frowned. "There weren't all that many New Sumatrans left by the time he was done."

They fell silent as the tram passed by once more.

"What's actually happened on New Sumatra, anyway?" asked Crane. "I had the computer retrieve the newstapes, but I haven't had a chance to go over them yet."

"There were 47,000 colonists on New Sumatra," said Pagliacci, his face expressionless beneath the clown's make-up. "An incredibly virulent disease hit us, some kind of mutated virus, and killed 12,000 of us before our medics managed to identify it. A scientific team on Sirius V finally synthesized an antidote and shipped it to New Sumatra. We knew it would take about two weeks to arrive, and in the meantime we isolated the colonists who had contracted the disease so that it couldn't spread, since it frequently took less than two weeks to kill. We set up a pair of hospital camps a considerable distance from the population centers, and waited for the medication. It arrived on time." He paused, and now the muscles in his jaws began twitching visibly. "But two days before it arrived, Bello ordered an air strike on each camp and destroyed every living soul in them." He paused again. "I suppose I should be more grateful than I am. I used to be a mediocre businessman; now I'm a first-rate killer."

Crane remained silent for what he felt was a proper length of time, and then spoke.

"Why didn't you kill him then and there?"

"He put the entire world under martial law, and then surrendered to the Navy when it arrived." Pagliacci grimaced. "I thought justice was being done."

"So your organization was formed after he escaped from prison?"

Pagliacci nodded. "He had help. No one escapes from a top security prison on his own. We've taken care of most of the helpers, but Bello himself has eluded us."

"Until now."

"Until now. We figured out after awhile that if we killed everyone who had shown any loyalty to him we'd never be able to get a line on his whereabouts, so we decided to leave half a dozen of his supporters—mostly military officers—under covert observation. Morales was mine."

"But he wasn't an officer."

"No—but he prepared a video presentation for Bello's lawyer, so we felt reasonably sure that he was sympathetic to Bello's cause."

"How did you know ten years ago that you'd have to be a nightclub performer to keep tabs on him?"

"I didn't," admitted Pagliacci. "But this identity allows me to hide, or at least mask, my facial features, and I can come and go freely to any world that I feel I have to visit."

"Your organization's got that much clout?" asked Crane.

"It's not as much as you think," replied Pagliacci. "We have extremely impressive credentials and we don't charge very much."

"We?" repeated Crane. "You're all clowns?"

"We're all entertainers."

"So your organization masquerades as a theatrical booking agency."

"I didn't say that."

"You didn't have to." Crane paused. "How long have you been keeping tabs on Morales?"

"Since we caught up with him about four years ago."

"Then why move now?" asked Crane. "Why the sudden pressure?"

"The Republic knows Bello is on Deluros VIII."

"Oh?"

"You look surprised. Don't be. The fact that they haven't been able to ferret him out in all this time isn't something they're very likely to broadcast." He paused. "Anyway, we learned from a lieutenant we captured that Morales was sent up here to arrange an escape route for Bello. At some unspecified point in time he was to transmit a message, Bello was to come up to the *Comet* on a shuttle flight, and a very fast ship would be waiting to take him to some new refuge."

"Then what was the point of killing Infante?" asked Crane, genuinely puzzled. "All it would have done would be to scare Morales off."

"This is a carefully orchestrated campaign," replied Pagliacci. "We're simultaneously putting all kinds of pressure on Bello's Deluros operatives. I wanted to convince Morales we were getting close to him, and force him to send that message while he still had the chance."

"Well, for a man who's a smart killer, you make an awfully dumb conspirator," replied Crane. "If Infante was the go-between, there's no way Bello could inform Morales that he's under siege."

"Morales knows. Bello's been under siege for six months."

"Even so, if this guy is half as loyal as you think, nothing in the universe is going to make him send that message. You should have waited until he felt safe."

"I couldn't," replied Pagliacci. "I leave the ship in another three weeks."

"Then you should have let the next guy handle it."

"Never!" said Pagliacci passionately. "He killed my wife and three daughters! I've spent ten years of my life tracking him down, and no one is going to rob me of my vengeance at the last moment!"

"Maybe we'd better get a couple of ground rules

straight here," said Crane, a note of concern in his voice. "On the unlikely assumption that Bello actually comes up to the *Comet*, my job is to capture him, not kill him. Vainmill doesn't need any more murders on this ship."

"Absolutely."

"Then why do I have the feeling that you're going to strangle him with your bare hands the second you see him?"

"I won't deny that I want to," admitted Pagliacci grimly. "But my job is also to bring him back to prison. People have already forgotten what happened on New Sumatra. Even a man as obviously well-informed as yourself no longer remembered the details. He's got to be taken back alive, and with maximum publicity, so that the Republic will never forget his crimes."

"At least for the next three or four years," commented Crane ironically.

"This time it will be different," said Pagliacci. "This time we'll have holographs of the trial and we'll have access to the court transcripts."

"Do you seriously think anyone's going to look at them or read them?"

"Yes, I do," answered Pagliacci. "Because we'll have something else we didn't have the last time around."

"Oh? What is that?"

"We'll have a genuine, bonafide hero, Andy," said Pagliacci. "We'll have *you*. You'll be fabled in song and story—and the songs and stories will all be about how you brought the Bloody Butcher to justice."

"I suppose I could learn to live with that," replied Crane with a tiny smile.

"Somehow I knew you could."

"But before you turn me into a video idol," continued Crane, "we've still got a little problem: namely, that I think you blew it when you tried to frighten Morales."

Pagliacci shook his head. "I had hoped he would send the message out of fear, or a sense of urgency, but now we'll simply have to apply another method."

"Did you have one in mind?"

"Compulsion."

"He's probably been conditioned to withstand anything you can dish out," replied Crane.

"But not anything *you* can dish out," said Pagliacci.

"I don't think I follow you."

"You're an executive with the Vainmill Corporation, Andy. That means you probably have access to a lot of places on this ship that are off-limits to a nightclub comic."

"Such as?"

"Such as the hospital's medical storeroom," replied Pagliacci with a grin. "It shouldn't take much effort on your part to find some nice will-sapping drug there—I've seen it used on a couple of violent drunks—and then we'll just pay Morales a visit, fuck around with his bloodstream for a few minutes, and tell him to send his message. It's got to be coded, so Bello will never know what condition our boy is in."

"Niathol," said Crane.

"What?"

"Niathol. That's the name of the drug." Crane walked out onto the floor of the tunnel. "Well, let's get to work. I just hope to hell you're right about Morales *transmitting* the message rather than sending it back with Infante."

"That's what our information says," replied Pagliacci. "Besides, we'll know in another hour or two if it was right." He checked his chronometer. "I've got to give another show in half an hour. Let's get the hell out of here before that damned tram comes back and runs us down."

The detective nodded and began walking. "I'll pick you up at the club after I get the niathol."

"Maybe I'll hit you with my detective routine after all," chuckled Pagliacci.

"You do, and the deal's off," said Crane unsmilingly.

9.

Crane had just removed a tiny container of niathol from a refrigeration unit in the hospital, and was searching for a syringe when the intercom system came to life.

"Mr. Crane?" said the Dragon Lady's voice.

He walked over to a terminal and activated it, and her holograph was projected a few feet in front of him.

"Yes?" he said.

"I wonder if you could come to my office?"

"Right now?" he replied. "I'm kind of busy."

"It's rather important."

"All right. I'll be there in five minutes."

He broke the connection, left a message for Pagliacci that he might be a few minutes late, hunted up a syringe, and took the slidewalk to the Home.

It took him no more than a minute to take the elevator up two levels and walk down the hall to her office. The door opened as he approached it and promptly slid shut behind him.

He had seen the room when he had spoken to her via holograph, but this was the first time he had actually been inside it. One wall housed an ancient, hand-carved wooden bookcase containing a very thorough tape and disk library, as well as one of the *Comet's* omnipresent wet bars, while a number of paintings, some of them alien in origin, covered the other walls. Her chrome desk was plain and utilitarian, as were the three chairs that faced it. There was a bank of computer terminals a few feet to the left of the desk, but only one screen that he could see. Everything seemed neat, well-organized, and uncluttered.

The Dragon Lady, wearing another burgundy robe, was seated behind her desk.

"What's up?" asked Crane, sitting down opposite her. "Has somebody made an attempt to get to Morales?"

"Not yet." She paused. "I think they will soon, though. That's what I wanted to talk to you about."

"*They*?"

She nodded. "Oh, yes, Mr. Crane. I suspect we're dealing with more than one person here."

"You do?"

"Yes. And by the way, you don't need a syringe for niathol. It can be administered orally."

"The bastard would probably bite a couple of my fingers off," replied Crane calmly. "I'll stick with the syringe, if it's all the same to you."

"Aren't you surprised that I know about the niathol?" she asked.

He shook his head. "I'd be surprised if you didn't." He smiled. "I spotted the cameras in the tunnel."

"You *did* tell me to improve our security."

"I know."

"Would you have told me about Pagliacci if I *hadn't* ordered the cameras to be placed there last night?"

"Not a chance," he responded. "That would prove you were too stupid or too careless to trust with the information." He paused. "I hope to hell that you didn't get me all the way over here just to brag about how competent you are."

"I got you here because a serious problem exists, and I want to know how you plan to handle it," said the Dragon Lady.

"I'll give the niathol to Morales, get him to send the message, and arrest Bello as soon as he arrives."

"*That* isn't the problem," she replied. "We've still got a murderer walking around the ship."

"Pagliacci? He's not going anywhere."

"He's a killer."

"He's all through killing. He wants Bello alive as much as I do."

"That doesn't make him any less of a murderer," she pointed out. "He's already killed Infante."

"This thing is a lot bigger than Infante," said Crane.

"I don't think I'm making myself clear," she persisted. "Pagliacci is, by his own admission, a murderer. Possibly he's even deranged. You have no way of knowing that his story is true."

"First of all, he's *not* a murderer."

"Oh? What is he, then?"

"In the strictest sense, I suppose he's a military executioner."

"What army does he work for, Mr. Crane?"

"None that any court will ever recognize," admitted Crane.

"Then arrest him," said the Dragon Lady.

"I gave him my word."

"Why do you think you have to keep a promise to a murderer?" she continued. "You can't be counting on him to help you identify Bello; surely the man has a new face and a new identity after all these years."

"I know."

"And yet you're going to let him go free, just because you gave your word?" she demanded.

"No," he replied with the hint of a smile. "I never promised that I wouldn't arrest him, just that I'd team up with him to capture Bello. Once that's accomplished, our deal is over."

She looked surprised. "Then you never had any intention of letting him go!"

"My job is capturing killers, not pointing them toward safe havens," he replied. "Besides, he's our insurance policy."

"Insurance policy?" she repeated, puzzled.

He nodded. "Bello might smell a trap and stay on Deluros, or he might slip right through our fingers before we can identify him. I can't go home empty-handed." He paused. "Pagliacci's really not a threat to anyone aboard the *Comet*, your doubts notwithstanding—but he *has* told me everything I need to know; and the more I think about it, the more I feel that the safest place for him is in a detention cell."

"I thought you gave him your word," she said sardonically.

"I did. That's why *you're* going to arrest him."

"Have I mentioned before that you're a very interesting person, Mr. Crane?"

"No—but I fully concur." He reached his arms above his head and stretched. "Well, I might as well go back to the club and get Pagliacci."

"Shall I come along?" she asked.

He shook his head. "No reason to. You're sure as hell not going to arrest him there. It would probably be better if you waited right here."

"What about meeting you in Morales' room?"

"We *could* arrest him in Morales' room, of course," said Crane. "But it makes more sense to let him walk here on his own power rather than drag him back at gunpoint. There's less chance for a mishap that way."

"Why should he be willing to come to my office?"

"Because he'll have no reason to be suspicious. After all, it'll give *your* career a hell of a boost if you can be in on the capture of Quintus Bello."

"You have no objection if I monitor the two of you when you're with Morales?"

"None at all," replied Crane. He got to his feet. "I think I'd better get going."

"I'll see you later."

He went down to the tramway entrance, took the tramcar to the Resort, and arrived at the nightclub just in time to see Pagliacci taking his bows. The comedian joined him a moment later.

"Everything set?" he asked.

Crane nodded. "We're ready to go."

"I got your message," said Pagliacci. "What was the hold-up?"

"A minor problem came up." Crane smiled. "You've got *two* partners now."

Pagliacci stopped walking. "What do you mean?"

"I had to let the Dragon Lady in on this."

"Why?" demanded Pagliacci.

"Because we're going to need her help," explained Crane. "We need a place to put Bello once we've got him. Until I know the ship is secure, I'm not going to chance walking him to the airlock. He could have a confederate aboard, or a patron might recognize him and try to play hero. Besides, she can monitor Morales' room, so we're not going to be able to keep this thing a secret anyway."

"I don't like it."

"There's nothing to worry about," Crane assured him. "It's in her own best interest to be in on the capture of Quintus Bello."

"And what about me?" asked Pagliacci.

"I don't know what you mean."

"I get very nervous when you pretend to be stupid, Andy," said Pagliacci. "What does she propose to do about me?"

"I told her that we had an agreement."

"She'd damned well better honor it."

They took the tram to Morales' room in silence. There was only one guard on duty, and Crane approached him.

"We're here to see the prisoner," he announced. "Please let us in."

"I'll have to clear it with the Dragon Lady," replied the guard.

"Make it fast," said Pagliacci. "We're in a hurry."

The guard glared at him, then pulled out a communicator and quickly received permission to let them pass into the room.

Morales, who had been laying on his bed, got to his feet when they entered.

"You're the guy who interviewed me," he said accusingly when he recognized Crane.

"That's right."

"Are you about ready to tell me what's going on here?"

"I had rather hoped you might tell me," replied the detective.

"Infante was my friend, damn it! I didn't kill him!"

"I know that," said Crane.

"Then why have I been incarcerated here?" demanded Morales.

"We're interested in another of your friends," said the detective.

"Who?"

"Quintus Bello."

"I never heard of him."

"*He's* heard of *you*," said Pagliacci easily.

"What the hell is *he* doing here?" demanded Morales, jerking his head in Pagliacci's direction.

"You want the truth?" asked Crane.

"Of course."

"He's here to kill you if you don't cooperate with me," said Crane casually. He nodded to Pagliacci, who withdrew his tiny handgun and pressed it up against Morales' head while Crane filled the syringe, painstakingly found a vein, and injected the drug into it.

Morales uttered a nonstop stream of curses for a moment, then suddenly slumped back, motionless.

"I hope to hell you didn't kill him," said the comedian, pocketing his gun and taking Morales' pulse.

"He's fine," replied Crane. "I've used this stuff before. He'll open his eyes in another minute or two, and then we can go to work."

"You're *sure* he's okay?" asked Pagliacci as Morales began trembling violently.

Before Crane could answer Morales sat up abruptly, blinking furiously.

"Esteban, my name is Crane," said the detective calmly. "Do you recognize me?"

"I know you," said Morales in a calm, conversational tone of voice.

"And this is Pagliacci," continued Crane. "You know him too, don't you?"

"Sure. He's a comedian."

"That's right," said Crane. "And of course you know that we're both your friends."

"Are you?" asked Morales innocently.

"Absolutely. Would you like us to prove it?"

"That would be nice."

"Fine," said Crane. "We'll be happy to. Is there any favor we can do for you?"

"I'm very thirsty," said Morales pleasantly. "I think I'd like a glass of water."

Crane nodded to Pagliacci, who went off to the bathroom to get one.

"Thank you," said Morales when the comedian returned.

"Doing favors for friends gives us a good feeling," said Crane. "Can we do another—a big one?"

"If you'd like," said Morales, sipping his water with a happy smile on his face.

"We'd like to do this one for a mutual friend."

"Oh? Who?"

"Quintus Bello."

Morales frowned. "I don't think you're supposed to know him."

"It's all right," said Crane soothingly. "We're his friends. We want to help him."

Morales seemed to consider the statement. "All right," he said after a few seconds.

"He's in danger if he stays on Deluros VIII," continued Crane. "His enemies are closing in on him. They'll capture him by tomorrow."

Morales began weeping. "That makes me very unhappy," he explained between sobs.

"That's why we want to help him," said Crane. "We want to tell him that it's time to come up to the *Velvet Comet*."

"His ship's not here yet," said Morales.

"He can use ours," said Crane.

Morales smiled. "That's very nice of you."

"Well, we like to be nice to our friends. But we have a problem."

"What is it?" asked Morales. "Maybe I can help."

"We don't know how to get in touch with him and tell him that it's time to come. Can you tell us how to do that?"

"No!" yelled Morales. "That's *my* job! Nobody else can tell him!"

"Then maybe you'd better tell him right away," said Crane smoothly. "After all, that's what friends are for."

Morales looked disturbed. "I don't know . . ." he mumbled.

"You *have* to," said Crane in soft, persuasive tones. "If you don't, he'll be captured by his enemies, and you know what they'll do to him."

"Kill him?"

"That's right. And we can't let our friend be killed, can we?"

"No."

"Then we'd better contact him right now."

"Just *me*," said Morales stubbornly.

"Just you," said Crane quickly. "But you don't

mind if we stay and visit for awhile, do you? After all, we're your friends."

Morales seemed to consider the suggestion. "I'm not sure," he said at last.

"But we insist," said Crane firmly.

Morales seemed to lose a struggle with himself. "Sure you can stay," he said with a smile. "You're my friends."

Crane activated the computer.

"It's all set for you," he said. "Pagliacci and I will stand in the farthest corner of the room so that we can't overhear you."

"That seems fair," agreed Morales pleasantly. He waited until the two men had walked to the corner, then turned to the computer and muttered something in a low whisper.

"That's it?" asked Crane.

Morales nodded happily. "Now we can visit."

"We'd love to," said Crane. "But you look very sleepy."

"I do?"

"Yes. Your eyelids are so heavy you can't keep them open."

Morales closed his eyes.

"Lay back on the bed and get some sleep," said Crane gently. "We'll come by and visit after you wake up."

Morales laid his head back on the pillow and muttered something unintelligible, and was sleeping peacefully a moment later.

Crane approached the computer.

"Cupid, who did he send that message to?"

IT WAS SENT TO A DUMB TERMINAL AT A MESSAGE DROP.

"Can you find out who rented it?"

WORKING . . . IT WAS RENTED BY SULIMAN HADIZ. I HAVE CHECKED HIS NAME AND ADDRESS AGAINST ALL DELUROS VIII DIRECTORIES, BUT CAN FIND NO LISTING.

"Not exactly surprising," commented Crane. "What was the text of the message?"

QUOTE: LET HE WHO IS WITHOUT SIN CAST THE FIRST STONE.

"Thanks. You can deactivate now." He turned to Pagliacci. "A phony name, a phony address, and a coded message. Just about what you'd expect."

"Then let's wake him up and get him to tell us where we can find Bello's headquarters. The man is going to be leaving a lot of lieutenants behind."

Crane shook his head. "It won't work."

"Why not?" demanded Pagliacci.

"Even with all that of niathol in him, he wouldn't let anyone else send the message. The man's been conditioned; he'll kill himself before he'll tell us where to find his headquarters."

"He thinks we're his friends."

"And even so, he wouldn't let us send a coded message to a dumb terminal. There's no way he's going to give us an address."

"What if you gave him a bigger dose of niathol?" asked Pagliacci.

"Then there'll be two killers in this room instead of one," said Crane with finality. He walked to the door. "Come on."

Pagliacci cast one last glance at the sleeping Morales, then fell into step behind Crane.

"Lock it," Crane ordered the guard when they were in the corridor. "Nobody comes or goes without my express orders." He jerked a thumb toward Pagliacci. "That includes *him*."

"I take my orders from the Dragon Lady," replied the guard. "Will she confirm this?"

"She will," said Crane, heading off to the elevator bank. "And when you talk to her, tell her we're on our way."

They took an elevator up to the Security level, then walked to the Dragon Lady's office.

She was sitting at her desk, waiting for them.

"I'm always impressed by what a little niathol can do," she said by way of greeting.

"It's an impressive drug," agreed Pagliacci, flashing her a smile and pulling up a chair. "Maybe I ought to shoot a dose into my friend Andy here, and convince him that I'm really not a bad comedian."

She ignored his remark and turned to Crane. "How long do you think it will take Bello to get up here?"

"No more than 72 hours," replied Crane. "Possibly a lot less. After all, I *did* tell Morales that Bello was in immediate danger. For all I know, there were two or three different messages he could send, and this was the most urgent of them."

"That's not very likely," interjected Pagliacci seriously. "An agent aboard the *Comet* isn't likely to be in a position to know whether or not Bello is in trouble. My guess is that he only had one message."

"Probably you're right," agreed Crane. "All we can do is hope Bello takes the bait."

"The Resort's suites are totally booked for the next three weeks," said the Dragon Lady, "so he'll most likely come up as a day-tripper, either on a shopping spree or a gambling binge."

"I just hope he'll make it easy on us and try to contact Morales," said Pagliacci.

Crane shook his head. "I doubt it," he said dubiously. "The man hasn't stayed free all these years by being stupid. They've either got a pre-arranged meeting place somewhere in the Mall or the Resort, or else he'll simply go to where he thinks his ship is docked. About the only thing we can be sure of is that he'll be coming up on a shuttle flight: if he had access to a ship in one of the orbiting hangars, he wouldn't have to arrange an escape route through the *Comet*." He paused. "Besides, they'd never give him clearance to take it just a few thousand miles to the *Comet*; there's already too much traffic congestion around Deluros VIII."

"May I make a suggestion?" said Pagliacci.

"Go ahead," replied Crane.

"Since we're not sure when he's arriving, I think we'd better arrange for each of us to keep a pair of four-hour watches each day. It doesn't make sense for all three of us to be asleep at the same time."

"I agree," said the Dragon Lady. "But I think we'll make it *three* four-hour watches."

"That comes to 36 hours," said Pagliacci.

"24," she corrected him. "Twelve for Mr. Crane and twelve for myself."

"Maybe Andy didn't tell you that he and I have a deal."

"I know," replied the Dragon Lady. "But you and I don't."

He looked amused. "You think you're going to arrest me?"

"I know I am," she replied calmly. "There are four

security men waiting for you on the other side of that door."

"Then I strongly suggest you tell them to go away," said Pagliacci. "Nobody's arresting anybody."

"You think not?"

"Not if you've got a brain in your head," said the comedian. "I'm willing to take my chances in a court of law—but are *you* willing to have me state under oath that not only did the staff of the *Comet* hush up a murder, but that you also lured the Bloody Butcher of New Sumatra onto the premises without warning any of your patrons?"

"Then we'll simply have to incarcerate you aboard the *Comet* until Bello has stood trial and been sentenced to jail."

He laughed. "How long will you keep me here—a year? Two years? Five? Do you really think what I have to say will be any less damaging then than now?"

"Perhaps."

He shook his head. "For that matter, do you think this is the only whistle I can blow? The sole criterion for admittance to the Resort is money; what do you suppose your patrons would say if they knew how some of the people they're rubbing shoulders with *make* their money? There are five professional killers aboard this ship right now; *I'm* only a talented amateur." He turned to Crane. "Maybe you'd better tell her that arresting me won't exactly be a boon to business, Andy."

"I know it won't," said Crane. "We'll just have to live with it."

"Yeah?" grinned Pagliacci. "And just how long do you think Vainmill will live with their hotshot detective once they figure out how much business he's cost their showplace operation?"

Crane and the Dragon Lady stared at each other.

"What do you think, Mr. Crane?" she said at last.

"He's right," said Crane.

"About your future?"

"About *my* future, and about the *Comet's*."

She sighed in resignation. "I know."

"Well, *that's* settled," said Pagliacci easily. "Everyone's allowed one mistake, and now you've made yours." Suddenly his voice became ominous. "See to it that you don't make any more, or we may all regret it." He got to his feet. "I assume that this is the real reason I was invited here, and that you've got nothing further to say to me?"

"Right," admitted Crane.

"And I thought we were going to be such good friends, Andy," he said with mock regret. He walked to the door, then turned to them. "Let me know when you've scheduled my two daily watches—and try not to have them conflict with the act."

"You're going to keep working in the club?" asked Crane, surprised.

"Why not? For all I know, Bello may send an advance man to check things out. Why call attention to myself?"

He walked out the door.

"Hey, Dragon Lady!" he called an instant later.

"Let him go," she ordered her security team.

The door slid shut behind him.

"He may be a bastard," said Crane, "but he's a *smart* bastard. I think we'd better move Morales to the hospital immediately."

"Why?"

"Because I don't want to call attention to *my*self, either. I'm supposed to be taking my prisoner to Deluros in the morning. If I'm going to stay aboard the *Comet*, I've got to have a reason. Have Cupid pass the word that Morales had a burst appendix, underwent emergency surgery, and can't be moved for a couple of days. That gives me an excuse to stick around."

"And what about Pagliacci?" she asked.

"The son of a bitch has us over a barrel," admitted Crane.

"You don't seem especially distressed by it," she noted disapprovingly.

"Nobody ever became chairman of Vainmill by arresting a hero," said Crane wryly.

"He's not a hero. He's a killer."

"He's a minnow. Let's start worrying about the whale."

10.

"Cupid?"

YES?

"You heard everything that was said in Morales' room and the Dragon Lady's office, I presume?"

OF COURSE.

"Got any ideas who the hell Pagliacci really is?"

A COMPUTER DOES NOT GENERATE IDEAS.

"Let me rephrase that," said Crane, leaning back on his contour chair. "Is there any evidence to imply who might have killed the real Stanley Dombroski?"

NONE.

"You checked it that fast?" asked Crane, surprised.

NO. BUT WHEN I HEARD PAGLIACCI CONFESS THAT HE HAD KILLED DOMBROSKI, I IMMEDIATELY BEGAN ACCESSING ALL PERTINENT INFORMATION.

"I thought computers didn't generate ideas," said the detective wryly.

THIS WAS NOT, STRICTLY SPEAKING, AN IDEA. BUT THAT PORTION OF MY INTELLIGENCE

WHICH IS PROGRAMMED FOR SECURITY HAS A COMPULSION TO SOLVE PROBLEMS.

"And seek the truth?"

YES.

"Interesting," commented Crane. He paused for a moment. "And you come up absolutely empty on the murder of Dombroski?"

STRICTLY SPEAKING, THERE IS NO PROOF THAT STANLEY DOMBROSKI WAS MURDERED.

"I think we can take Pagliacci's word for it."

I AGREE.

"Value judgements, too?"

PROBABILITY ANALYSIS. I CAN, HOWEVER, MAKE VALUE JUDGEMENTS, GIVEN SUFFICIENT DATA.

"I don't doubt it," said Crane. "Let's try one shot in the dark, and then give up on it: did Dombroski ever perform on New Sumatra?"

NO.

"Then trying to figure out who Pagliacci really is makes looking for a needle in a haystack seem easy. We'll just have to deal with him as he is."

He got up, poured himself a cup of coffee, and returned to his chair.

"How long has it been since Morales sent the message?"

11 HOURS, 27 MINUTES. YOU ARE SCHEDULED TO BE ON WATCH AGAIN IN 33 MINUTES.

"It won't do a bit of good."

IS THERE SOME REASON WHY NOT?

"Because none of us knows what Bello is going to look like. The only physical feature that won't be changed is his height, and he'll probably be stooped over or wearing lifts in his shoes or something like that."

THEN WHY BOTHER KEEPING WATCH AT ALL?

Crane sighed. "Because I don't know what else to do, short of turning Morales loose and keeping an eye on him."

THAT SEEMS A REASONABLE PROCEDURE. IS THERE SOME REASON WHY YOU REFUSE TO DO IT?

"Of course there is."

MAY I KNOW THE REASON?

"Because if I don't dope him up, he'll find some way to blow the whistle to Bello before we can spot him . . . and if I shoot him full of niathol, Bello will know we've gotten to him."

HOW, IF YOU CONVINCE HIM THAT AN ESCAPE SHIP IS REALLY WAITING?

"Because he won't give me the details of how they plan to make contact, and without that Bello will reach him before I reach Bello." He grunted irritably. "So I guess that all we can do is watch for Bello and hope we know him when we see him." He finished his coffee. "Connect me with the Dragon Lady."

The Security Chief's image appeared instantly.

"Any luck?" he asked.

"None," she replied. "I keep wondering if Pagliacci knows more than he's telling us."

"Such as?"

"Such as what Bello will look like."

"I doubt it," replied Crane. "That would imply he'd seen him recently, and I can't imagine they'd both still be alive if that was the case."

"I hope you're right," said the Dragon Lady. "Anyway, we've checked out nine shoppers and five gamblers who arrived without reservations, and all of them seem legitimate."

"All right. I'll spell you in half an hour."

"I can remain on duty for a few more hours if you'd like to take a nap or stop by one of the restaurants."

He shook his head. "I'm not sleepy, and I can have my meals brought to me."

"You're sure?"

Crane frowned. "Just how sleepy and hungry do I look?"

"Not very," admitted the Dragon Lady. "But I know how little rest you've had since arriving . . ."

"I'll rest after we've nailed Bello."

He broke the connection, then walked to the bathroom, stared into a mirror, and realized that he *did* look a bit haggard. He quickly shaved, then ordered Cupid to activate the whirlpool while he got out of his clothes and laid a fresh set out in the bedroom.

"Too damned hot," he muttered, when he had immersed his body in the whirlpool.

THE TEMPERATURE IS 42 DEGREES CELSIUS. WHAT TEMPERATURE WOULD YOU LIKE?

"Oh, make it about 36 or 37," replied Crane.

He leaned back, propping his head up against the edge of the circular tub.

"This screen," he said, indicating the device in front of a tiled wall, "—is it just for communicating with you, or can I get a holographic image on it?"

ALL SCREENS IN THE GUEST SUITES ARE HOLOGRAPHIC.

"All right," he said. "I want to clear my mind for the next few minutes and come back to this thing refreshed. Let me see one of the entertainment channels."

I HAVE 134 ENTERTAINMENT CHANNELS. WHICH ONE WOULD YOU PREFER?

"Whatever you think I'll enjoy."

I DON'T BELIEVE I AM QUALIFIED TO MAKE THAT JUDGEMENT.

"Try!" snapped Crane. "Just don't bother me."

WORKING . . .

Suddenly the writing vanished, to be replaced by a holograph of an enormous, satin-covered, circular bed. The Black Pearl, totally nude except for a thin gold chain around her waist, was laying on her back, while two athletic young men, equally nude, were busily kissing and stroking her.

Crane watched, fascinated, as the three writhed and rolled across the bed. He knew at a glance that the magnificently-endowed man on her right had to be the aptly-named Totem Pole, and he recognized the other as one he had seen once or twice in the casino in the company of an elderly, jewel-laden woman.

The action in the holograph became more frenzied as the Black Pearl used her hands, her mouth, and everything else she possessed to spur her partners on to greater efforts. Crane had seen pornographic cinemas and holographs before, but never had he encountered one that was performed with such grace, such lack of awkwardness, such pure animal eroticism.

He wanted to tell Cupid to wipe the image from the screen, or deactivate entirely, but he couldn't tear his eyes from the madam as she lithely moved from one position to another, finding more and more ways to accommodate both her partners at once.

"Change the goddamned channel!" he said finally, just as all three participants were about to climax.

The image changed instantly, and now he was confronted by the Black Pearl, her smooth skin glistening with oil, performing a sensuous dance to the pulsating, insistent rhythm of an alien symphony. As the beat became faster, she metamorphosed from a sleek terpsichorean to a grinning wanton, and the dance slowly changed from erotic to obscene.

"*Enough!*"

The screen went blank.

"What's the big idea?"

COMPUTERS DO NOT ORIGINATE IDEAS.

"You know what I mean. Why did you show me the Black Pearl?"

YOU TOLD ME TO SHOW YOU WHAT YOU WOULD ENJOY. YOU ENJOY THE BLACK PEARL.

"Not that way, I don't!"

MY MONITORING OF YOUR VARIOUS PHYSICAL FUNCTIONS LEADS ME TO CONCLUDE THAT YOU ENJOY HER PRECISELY THAT WAY.

"Shut up."

The screen went blank.

"Is that the only entertainment you've got?" demanded Crane at last.

I HAVE 132 OTHER CHANNELS.

"Then you must have some songs or dances or cinemas."

I JUST SHOWED YOU A DANCE.

"Something that isn't pornographic."

A ballet, obviously recorded in one of the huge

theaters on Deluros VIII, suddenly appeared. Crane tried to concentrate on it for a moment, then leaned back and sighed.

"Forget it. I'm not in the mood anymore."

WOULD YOU LIKE ANOTHER ENTERTAINMENT WITH THE BLACK PEARL? I HAVE 83 MORE IN MY LIBRARY.

"No!" shouted Crane, rising and clambering out of the whirlpool. "Where the hell's a towel?"

IF YOU WILL STAND APPROXIMATELY 2 FEET TO YOUR LEFT, I WILL HEAT-DRY YOU.

"I want a towel."

HEAT-DRYING IS FASTER AND MORE EFFICIENT.

"I'd rather do it myself," said Crane.

IS THERE SOME REASON WHY?

"I'm mad at you."

BECAUSE OF MY SHOWING YOU THE BLACK PEARL?

"Will you just get me a fucking towel, or am I supposed to stand here until I drip-dry?"

A row of six wall tiles slid to one side, revealing a drawer that automatically glided open. Crane walked over, picked up a bath towel, and began drying himself off. When he was through he ordered the computer to clean and deactivate the bathroom while he walked into the bedroom and got dressed.

Finally he walked back to the living area, sat down on the contour chair, and leaned back.

"Activate."

The screen came to life.

"Let me see the airlock."

The airlock appeared.

"Empty," muttered Crane. "All right. Start scanning the Mall and close in on all the male day-trippers. Go back to the airlock only when someone actually arrives there."

The scene suddenly shifted to the Mall, and the camera homed in on a blond, somewhat overweight young man who was just emerging from a jewelry store, a brightly-wrapped package in his hand.

"Too small," said Crane. "And probably too young. Let's try another."

He spent the next half hour scrutinizing various shoppers and gamblers. Then, when he had examined them all, he ordered the computer to put the airlock on permanent display.

Another twenty minutes passed, and then the screen went blank.

CAN YOU ACCEPT AN INTRA-SHIP COMMUNICATION, OR SHALL I TELL THE CALLER TO WAIT UNTIL YOU ARE OFF-DUTY?

"Nothing much is happening," replied Crane. "You might as well patch it through."

Suddenly the Black Pearl's image appeared before him.

"Good afternoon, Mr. Crane."

"Good afternoon," he replied, wondering if the computer were monitoring his pulse and heartbeat.

"I wonder if you could stop by my office in the next ten minutes or so?" she asked. "*Alone*."

He hated to think of what that last word had done to his blood pressure.

"Why?" he said at last.

"There's someone here who very much wants to make your acquaintance," answered the Black Pearl.

"Oh? Who?"

"His name is Quintus Bello."

11.

A two-way intercom system clicked on as Crane stood before the Black Pearl's door, waiting for it to open.

"Are you armed?" asked the madam.

"No."

There was a momentary pause.

"Cupid, is he armed?"

Another pause.

"You lied to me, Mr. Crane," said the Black Pearl, sounding less than surprised. "Cupid tells me that you have a pistol hidden on your person. You'll have to get rid of it before I let you in."

"Thanks a lot, pal," muttered Crane. He walked to the end of the corridor, signaled to a nearby security man, and handed the pistol over to him, simultaneously ordering him to remain in the general vicinity of the Black Pearl's office.

He then walked back to the door.

"All right," he said.

"Has he gotten rid of it, Cupid?" she asked. Evidently the computer confirmed his status, for a moment later the door slid into the wall and Crane stepped into the Black Pearl's office.

"Where is he?" demanded the detective.

"He's in with my Night Crystals," she replied calmly. "I'll call him out in a moment."

"What the hell are Night Crystals?"

"That's not important," said the Black Pearl. "What *is* important is that we reach an understanding before I let you talk to Bello."

"What kind of understanding?" he asked suspiciously.

"Nobody knows he's on the *Comet*. I want it to stay that way."

"Fine. He won't be on it that long, anyway. I'll have him back on Deluros inside of four hours."

"No, you won't," she said firmly. "Nobody's arresting anyone until *I* decide its necessary."

"*What?*" he exploded. "Do you know who he is?"

"And what he's done," she replied, nodding her head. "But I have the distinct impression that you've been holding out on me, Mr. Crane."

"In what way?"

"I don't know, but I don't think he would be here if it weren't for you." She frowned. "You arranged to bring a very notorious man aboard *my* ship without telling me."

"Then let me take him right back off," urged Crane.

"I haven't made up my mind yet."

"Damn it—you're talking about a genocidal maniac!"

"I'm talking about the welfare of the *Comet*, which is the only thing that matters to me. I don't give a damn what Quintus Bello did or didn't do on New Sumatra. Now, do we have a deal or not?"

He glared at her for a moment, then shrugged and nodded tersely.

"That means yes?" she asked.

"Yes."

"Cupid, is he telling the truth?"

I AM NOT A LIE DETECTOR. HIS PULSE AND HEARTBEAT ARE VERY RAPID, BUT WHILE THAT COULD INDICATE HE IS LYING, IT MIGHT MERELY BE A MANIFESTATION OF HIS SEXUAL DESIRE FOR YOU.

"I'm going to kill that fucking machine!" muttered Crane, shifting his weight uneasily under the Black Pearl's amused gaze. Finally he stopped glaring at the screen and turned to her. "Well?" he said.

"I want you to put this meeting on your Priority File," she answered.

"You named your conditions, and I agreed to them. That wasn't one of them."

"I don't want the Security Department knowing about Bello's presence here."

"Well, I want the Dragon Lady to know. I'll put this on the Priority File only if I can access it for her later today."

She nodded. "All right."

He turned to the screen.

"Cupid, you back-stabbing son of a bitch—are you awake?"

YES.

"Has anyone been monitoring this conversation?"

NO.

"Put everything that's said in this office in my Priority File, and make it retroactive to the moment the Black Pearl contacted me in my suite."

WORKING . . . DONE.

"Also, where's Pagliacci right now?"

PAGLIACCI IS CURRENTLY PERFORMING IN THE NIGHTCLUB.

Crane turned back to the Black Pearl. "All right," he said.

She walked to a door at the back of the office, commanded it to open, said something he couldn't hear, and then stood aside as Quintus Bello entered the room.

He stood five feet nine inches, but appeared a bit smaller. His hair was white and thinning, his eyes blue-green, his nose straight and a bit oversized, his chin prominent and thrust forward. He walked with an erect, almost military, bearing, and carried very little excess flesh. His outfit identified him as a cargo hand from one of the freighters that brought the *Comet's* kitchens their daily supply of fresh food from Deluros VIII.

"Mr. Crane?" he said in a voice that was deeper than Crane had expected.

"That's right," said Crane, eyeing him warily.

"I suspect that you are the man who caused Esteban to send for me."

"What makes you think so?"

"Because I hadn't been on the ship for two minutes before I realized that Esteban Morales had either been tricked or forced into sending that message."

"You were supposed to meet him in the Mall?" asked Crane.

"At any rate," continued Bello, ignoring his remark, "the moment I knew that I had been duped, I determined that the madam of the ship would be the one person most likely to provide some form of asylum, and I immediately made my way here."

"What made you think she'd give you protection?"

A tiny smile flashed across Bello's face. "Come now, Mr. Crane," he said. "If you were bright enough to lure me up here, then surely you are bright enough to know why it is in the madam's best interest that I be allowed to go my own way."

"True," said Crane. "But I'm not the madam."

"So now we come to the crux of it," said Bello. "For what purpose am I here?"

"You're an escaped felon who has been convicted of genocide," said Crane. "Why do *you* suppose I tricked you up here?"

"I tell you now, Mr. Crane," said Bello in level tones, "that I will never submit to capture or imprisonment again."

"That, Mr. Bello," said Crane, "is a point of some debate."

"None," said Bello firmly. "I surrendered to the authorities fifteen years ago, and they betrayed me."

"Possibly because you betrayed 11,000 citizens who were under your protection," remarked Crane caustically.

'I did *not*—and no jury of my peers would ever convict me!"

"Probably not," agreed Crane.

Bello looked surprised. "Then you know the story?"

Crane shook his head. "No, but I imagine any jury composed of genocidal maniacs is pretty likely to let you off the hook."

Bello stared at him for a long moment, his face an inscrutable mask. Finally he spoke.

"Sit down, Mr. Crane."

"Only if you will," said Crane. "And I've got to sit closer to the door."

Bello nodded, and walked to one of the sofas. Suddenly he turned to the Black Pearl, who had been standing silently by the doorway leading to her Night Crystals. "Won't you please join us?"

"Why not?" she said with a shrug.

Bello moved over to make room for her, but she walked to Crane's sofa instead.

"I may save your neck," she said, "but I'd rather not sit next to you."

Bello nodded, seated himself, and waited for Crane to do the same. Then he leaned forward at stared intently at the detective.

"What, exactly, do you know about New Sumatra, Mr. Crane?" he said at last.

"I know that you were the governor of the planet for seven years, I know that some kind of mutated virus came along and started wiping out colonists by the thousands, I know that they finally developed a vaccine to cure the disease—and I know that you ordered air strikes on two hospital camps just before the vaccine arrived, killing more than 11,000 citizens whose welfare you were there to protect."

"And that is the extent of your knowledge?" said Bello.

"Just the highlights," said Crane. He ordered the computer to give a complete readout on the Bello Affair.

Bello watched emotionlessly, as the details of the affair appeared on the screen, then turned back to Crane when the computer had finally emptied its library banks on the subject.

"As I suspected," he said. "Half-truths and misinterpretations, nothing more."

"There's a native of New Sumatra onboard the

ship right now who will be only too happy to corroborate what you just read," remarked Crane.

"I'm sure he will," said Bello.

"Are you saying that the computer's account of what happened isn't true?" asked the Black Pearl.

"It's entirely true," said Bello. He paused. "As I pointed out at my trial, it's also completely wrong."

"You don't find that just a little inconsistent?" asked Crane.

"What do *you* know of it?" exploded Bello. "You weren't there! The disease was decimating the colony. 12,000 people were already dead, and 11,000 more were dying!"

"Are you trying to say that this was a mercy killing?" asked Crane incredulously.

"No!" said Bello impatiently, the muscles in his jaw twitching spasmodically. "It was a decision that was made to benefit the greatest number of people!"

"Perhaps you'd care to explain how killing 11,000 colonists benefited anyone," said Crane.

"The virus was airborne, wildly contagious, and absolutely fatal," said Bello, his eyes fixed on some spot in space and time that only he could see. "Very few people who contracted it lived more than 20 days, and most of them died hideous deaths; no drug we possessed could alleviate the excruciating pain of the final few days." He paused and sighed heavily. "We did everything we could, but we couldn't come up with a cure. The best we could do was try to contain it. I moved all the sick into two huge hospital camps, and put lethal electric fencing around it. Most of the doctors volunteered to keep working in the camps, since they had already been exposed to the disease." His voice softened. "And then we got word that someone on Sirius V had isolated the virus and developed an antidote. It was rushed into production and shipped out to us. The trip was supposed to take 15 days."

He fell silent for a moment, still staring blankly into space, then focused his eyes on Crane.

"Four days before the ship was due to arrive, we lost all radio contact with it. 36 hours later the Republic decided that it had broken down, and immediately dispatched another ship loaded with the antidote, on the assumption that it would take them too much time to find a ship that had malfunctioned at light speeds and whose cargo might well be beyond salvage."

He paused once more, searching Crane's face for some emotion, but finding none.

"Every shred of information I possessed convinced me that we could expect no help for another two weeks," he continued. "As far as I could see, not a single person in the hospital camps would survive until the arrival of the second ship—but the longer they lived, the more likelihood there was that we couldn't continue to contain the disease. No matter how isolated the camps were, they had to be supplied with food and medication. Sooner or later the thing had to start spreading again, so I carried out the proper procedure: I sacrificed those who were already lost in order to save the remainder of the colony."

There was a moment's silence.

"And then the ship arrived," said Crane.

Bello nodded. "Two days later." He frowned. "Their communications system had gone out."

"But they arrived," repeated Crane.

"Damn it!" snapped Bello. "No one could pick them up on sensing devices, and even the Republic pronounced them lost and presumed dead!"

"But they weren't."

"No, they weren't," agreed Bello angrily. "But I did what I had to do. I made the prescribed decision to achieve the greatest good—and given the information I had, I'd do it again!"

"It sounds reasonable," said the Black Pearl. "Why didn't the jury acquit you?"

"Because the Republic needed a scapegoat after news of what happened got out," said Bello. "And like a fool, I expected justice at their hands and gave myself up."

"And escaped," Crane pointed out.

"Not without help," said Bello. "Not without the aid of people who knew I'd been unjustly accused and convicted." He took a deep breath, released it slowly, and stared defiantly at Crane. "I won't go back, not until you can find a jury of twelve military governors who understand what the situation was."

"Military?" asked Crane, surprised.

Bello nodded. "There had been some initial trouble with the native population."

"During your tenure?"

"Long before I got there," replied Bello. "They were pacified, but it was felt that a military presence was necessary to remind them to leave human beings alone." He grimaced. "Wouldn't you know those little red bastards were totally immune to the disease!"

"You should have demanded a military trial," said Crane.

"I did. My request was refused, and the transcript of my trial was never released."

"Well, you can try again this time," said Crane.

"You still plan to arrest me?" asked Bello, unsurprised.

"I'm not a judge or a jury; I'm just a detective. You're an escaped felon who by his own admission killed 11,000 innocent men and women."

"11,000 *doomed* men and women," Bello corrected him.

"That's not the way it turned out," replied Crane.

"I made my decision based on the best information I possessed," said Bello. "I won't apologize for it."

"Have I asked you to?"

"And I won't play the scapegoat for it, either!"

"We all have our problems," said Crane. "This one happens to be yours."

"What would *you* have done?" demanded Bello.

"I don't know," admitted Crane.

"Then how dare you condemn me!"

"I'm not condemning you" said Crane patiently. "But I sure as hell intend to arrest you."

"I happen to know that you are not armed," said Bello ominously.

"Are you threatening to kill an unarmed man?" asked Crane. "I thought that was how you got into this mess in the first place."

Bello sighed and leaned back on the sofa.

"No," he said, "I'm not threatening to kill you. But I tell you again, I will never go back to jail."

"There are worse fates," commented Crane. "I could tell Pagliacci you're here, and you'll face the biggest kangaroo court you ever saw."

"Pagliacci?" repeated Bello. "Is he a clown or an opera singer?"

"Neither. He's a killer, and he's pretty good at his job."

"He's the New Sumatran?"

Crane nodded. "You killed his wife and his daughters."

"For all he knows, they were already dead," said Bello.

"For all *you* know, the antidote would have cured them," replied Crane.

"It wasn't that simple!" exploded Bello. "And I won't have you make it that simple! There was the rest of the colony to be considered. If I hadn't done what I did, there might not have been a person left alive three weeks later—not me, not this Pagliacci, not anyone!"

"*If* the ship hadn't arrived," noted Crane.

"I made the right decision based on the facts at hand!" stormed Bello. "It was the *only* decision under the circumstances, and I'd do it again!"

"So you've said," replied the detective.

Bello stared at him for a moment, then sighed. "I should have known better than to think you would understand," he said at last.

"You'll forgive me if I cling to the assumption that any man who slaughters 11,000 people is more sinning than sinned against," said Crane dryly.

Bello shook his head sadly. "Fool," he said. Then he sighed again. "We're *both* fools, Mr. Crane," he added wearily. "You for not comprehending what happened, and me for thinking that you might."

"Mr. Crane has other things on his mind just now," interjected the Black Pearl. "Parades through the streets, official commendations, promotions, pay raises . . . *so* many wonderful visions."

Both men turned to her.

"Mr. Crane," she continued, "is destined to be disappointed."

"You think so?" said Crane.

She nodded. "Mr. Bello has already promised never to mention his brief excursion aboard the *Comet* if I let him go. Can you make the same promise if I let him stay?"

"I already told you—" began Crane.

"I know what you told me," interrupted the Black Pearl. "But you haven't told me how you're going to shut him up once he gets into court—or did you plan to kill him right here on the *Comet*?"

"This is more important than the *Comet*," said Crane. "Don't you understand that we're talking about *Quintus Bello*?"

"*Nothing* is more important than the *Comet*," she replied firmly. "You show me how you can arrest him without harming our reputation and you can have him. In the meantime, he stays with me."

"And if he tries to escape?"

"May I point out that I don't have the means to escape?" interposed Bello. "I came here on the assumption that a ship would be waiting for me. It isn't."

"Not good enough," said Crane. "*I* could book passage on an outbound ship. Why can't you?—and please don't ask me to believe that you're traveling under your own name."

"Of course not."

"Well, then?"

"I give you my word," said Bello.

"You've already given me your word that you'll

never go back to prison," noted Crane. "Which one should I believe?"

"The two are not necessarily incompatible," replied Bello. "Simply let me go back to my headquarters on Deluros."

"Not a chance," said Crane.

"Then we're at an impasse," said Bello.

"Until I get my gun, anyway."

"I won't allow you in here again if you're carrying a weapon," said the Black Pearl.

"And I won't allow him out of here unless he's under arrest," replied Crane. "So Pagliacci and I will take turns sitting in the corridor watching your door. How long do you suppose it'll take before some of the patrons notice?" He could see concern on her face, and he pressed his advantage. "And while we're on the subject, what do you suppose it'll do for business if I announce that you're harboring a fugitive named Quintus Bello in your apartment and won't turn him over to me?"

She relaxed suddenly.

"You should have quit while you were ahead, Mr. Crane," she replied calmly. "You won't do anything that will jeopardize your job. Having Mr. Bello's presence inadvertently discovered is one thing; announcing it to 500 patrons is another."

"Don't be so sure of that," he said. "The man who captures Bello can write his own ticket."

"Not if you cost the *Velvet Comet* a few billion credits due to the publicity," she answered. "Oh, you'll be able to latch on somewhere else, but you'll have a black mark on your record, and my reading of your character is that you have every intention of going through life without any black marks."

"Sometimes they can't be helped."

"True. But this isn't one of those times, so you'll have to excuse me if I don't take your threat very seriously."

"You're not dealing just with me," said Crane. "If the Dragon Lady and Pagliacci don't know he's on the ship yet, they soon will. She's just a few years from retirement, and he's fighting a holy war. How are you going to keep them quiet?"

"I'll worry about them when the time comes," said the Black Pearl. "*You're* my problem at the moment."

"You're sitting in a room with a mass murderer, and *I'm* your problem?" said Crane with a bitter laugh.

"He never harmed my ship. *You* might."

"You've got a funny sense of values."

"Perhaps—but I didn't fuck five thousand totally forgettable men and women and claw my way to the top of the heap just to let some egomaniacal detective's ambition bring the whole operation tumbling down."

"We're getting nowhere," announced Bello. "Mr. Crane, what do you propose do to?"

"Arrest you."

"Like hell you will!" snapped the Black Pearl.

"Do you plan to arrest me right now?" persisted Bello.

"This minute?" asked Crane. "No."

"Then," said Bello, rising to his feet, "I think I'll take my leave of you. I don't like your company very much."

He walked, proudly and erectly, to the door at the back of the office, ordered it to open, and passed through into the room that contained the Night Crystals.

"Confident son of a bitch, isn't he?" remarked Crane. He turned to the Black Pearl. "Doesn't it bother you that he killed all those people?"

"No more, I think, than it bothers you " she replied. "Besides, he has a legitimate justification."

"So did Hitler and Caligula," noted Crane ironically. "Of all the people who survived New Sumatra, perhaps a dozen are loyal to him and there are thousands who want to kill him. Has it occurred to you that you've just heard a very subjective account of the whole affair, that the facts may be totally different?"

"If you knew he was telling the truth, would it make a difference?" asked the Black Pearl.

He shook his head. "I've been waiting for an opportunity like this all my life."

"Even if he's innocent?"

"He killed them, didn't he?"

"You know what I mean."

"Like I said, it's just my job to arrest him. Someone else will pass judgment."

"It won't work that way," she pointed out. "No judge who wants to live out the day will release him."

"That's not my problem, is it?" he said irritably.

"In a way, it is," she replied. "If you arrest him, it will be the same as condemning him to death."

"Perhaps—but if I arrest him, I'll be turning him over to the law. If I don't, I'll be taking it into my own hands. Besides," he added, "you're no more concerned with whether or not he's guilty than I am.

My job is to arrest him, and yours, it seems, is to try to stop me."

"You make it sound very stark."

"It is."

She stared at him for a moment. "I could sweeten the pot."

He arched an eyebrow. "How?"

"Let him go and you've got a free pass to my bedroom for as long as you want it. We'll do it whenever you want to, any way that you want to, as often as you want to."

He smiled at her. "Who suggested that—Cupid?"

"Have we got a deal?" she said, grinning confidently.

He shook his head, still smiling. "Not a chance."

"But—"

"You're asking me to trade the chance of a lifetime for something you give away every day," said Crane. "That's not much of a deal from where I sit."

"If you'd have Cupid show you some of the entertainments I've appeared in, you might feel differently about it."

"There are more important things in life than a roll in the hay."

"If everyone else aboard the *Comet* felt that way, I'd turn Bello over to you in a second," she said seriously. "But they don't, and I can't let you bring us so much adverse publicity that it frightens them away."

"How do you know it won't attract even more of them?" he replied. "People have always been fascinated by flirting with danger."

"Not *these* people," said the Black Pearl. "Even the poorest of them is a juicy target for kidnappers. The jewelry that's on the ship any given day would probably make a hefty down payment on the *Comet* itself. We guarantee security, and we don't allow weapons or bodyguards. Danger is just about the last thing our patrons are looking for—and if they *are* seeking it, they go to the fantasy rooms, where they can have all of the thrills of danger without any of the risks."

"Maybe," he acquiesced with a shrug. "But no matter what you and I decide, you're still not going to be able to keep a lid on this situation."

"You're referring to the Dragon Lady and Pagliacci?" asked the Black Pearl.

"Yes."

"She'll have enough brains to keep quiet—and as for *him*, why should he even know Bello is aboard the *Comet*?"

"He's not stupid," said Crane. "He was there with me when I gave Morales the niathol. He saw him send the message."

"So *that's* how you did it. Why wasn't I told?"

"Because it happened less than a day ago, and we've been keeping a round-the-clock watch on the airlock."

"So he fooled you by entering the service deck as a cargo mover, walked down to this end of the ship, and climbed up a service stairwell," she said mockingly. "Some detective!"

"Well, the plan did have a built-in handicap," admitted Crane. "None of us knew what Bello would look like."

"You mean you simply invited a mass murderer up to the *Comet* and hoped everything would work out all right?" she demanded.

"We had an opportunity to draw him out of hiding. We might never have had another."

"You deliberately endangered everyone on the *Comet*!"

"Nonsense. He's a fugitive. All he wants to do is get away."

"And you think fugitives don't kill when they feel they're endangered?"

"Everyone has the capacity to kill, just as they have the capacity to screw. You make your living from the one, I make mine from the other."

"You may be intelligent, and you may be as good at your job as you claim to be, Mr. Crane," she said angrily, "but you're a pretty poor excuse for a human being! You gambled my patrons' lives to advance your career, just as you're now gambling my ship and Bello's future."

"Whereas *you* are perfectly willing to let a mass murderer go free rather than risk some financial loss," he replied sardonically.

The Black Pearl got to her feet.

"I think it's time for you to leave, Mr. Crane," she announced. "I have nothing further to say to you."

He stood up and turned to the computer.

"Cupid?"

YES.

"Wait three minutes and then close the Priority File. Then instruct the Dragon Lady to access it on my authority."

UNDERSTOOD.

He turned back to the Black Pearl.

"This isn't over yet, you know," he said.

"I know."

"I can't let Bello walk away from here."

"Certainly you can—although my previous offer has been withdrawn," she added, staring at him distastefully.

"Sooner or later you're going to have to turn him over to me," said Crane.

"You're welcome to think so, Mr. Crane."

"You could make it easier on everyone if you'd do it now and get it over with."

"*Everyone*?" she repeated sarcastically. "Since when did you start caring about anyone except yourself?"

He stared at her, then walked to the door, which slid back into the wall.

"I'll be back," he promised.

"I'll be waiting," she replied in level tones.

12.

Crane retrieved his weapon, returned to his suite, and immediately activated the computer.

"Open the Priority File."

DONE.

"Is Bello still in the Black Pearl's apartment?"

YES.

"I'm ordering you to inform me the instant he tries to leave, either alone or in the Black Pearl's company."

UNDERSTOOD.

Crane lowered his head in thought for a moment, then looked up at the screen.

"If he tried to make it to the tramway right now, could I stop him?"

ALLOWING FOR NORMAL TRAFFIC PATTERNS, HE WOULD ARRIVE THERE ALMOST TWO MINUTES AHEAD OF YOU.

"Then I can't stay here any longer. Is there a vacant store within 200 feet of the airlock?"

ALL OF THE STORES ARE RENTED.

Crane frowned. "All right," he said. "The first

thing we'd better do is shut down the tramway. Then I'll move over to the Home, which is a lot closer to the airlock than the Resort is."

I CANNOT DEACTIVATE THE TRAMWAY SYSTEM EXCEPT ON THE AUTHORITY OF THE DRAGON LADY, PAXTON OGLEVIE, OR THE HEAD OF THE MAINTENANCE DEPARTMENT.

"Do you mean to say I can't close it down, even with my security clearance?"

THAT IS CORRECT.

"Okay. Connect me to the Dragon Lady."

SHE HAS ORDERED ME NOT TO INTERRUPT HER UNTIL SHE FINISHES VIEWING THE LATEST ADDITION TO YOUR PRIORITY FILE, WHICH YOU INSTRUCTED ME TO SHOW HER.

"Then get me Oglevie."

The screen went blank, to be replaced by Oglevie's image a moment later.

"Mr. Crane, sir," he said with a smile. "I haven't seen you for a couple of days. How are you, sir?"

"Just fine," said Crane. "I want you to do me a favor."

"If it's within my power."

"Shut down the tramway."

"For how long, sir?" asked Oglevie.

"Until I say otherwise."

"I'm not sure I can do that, sir," he said, obviously disturbed.

"The computer says you can."

"But the Black Pearl contacted me not two minutes ago and told me that you might make such a request, and that I should ignore it."

"It's not a request," said Crane. "It's an order."

Oglevie shifted uncomfortably. "Well, theoretically

the Black Pearl is the ultimate authority on the *Velvet Comet*. I don't think it would look very good on my record if I dismissed *her* order out of hand."

"*I'm* in charge of this investigation!" snapped Crane. "In case it's slipped your mind, you're working directly for me."

"But you've already arrested Esteban Morales for the murder of Edward Infante," said Oglevie. "Whatever is happening now, a case could be made that you are exceeding your authority." He paused. "Of course, if you could tell me what's happening, then maybe I—"

"I don't have to tell you a goddamned thing! Now, are you going to obey my orders or not?"

"I truly don't see how I can, sir."

"Well, if protecting your ass means that much to you, you do what you think is best," said Crane with a shrug.

"Thank you, sir," said Oglevie, looking much relieved.

"But let me tell you something," continued Crane.

"Sir?"

"You've just put your money on the wrong team. Twenty minutes from now the Dragon Lady is going to close down the tramway, and when I've finished what I've got to do up here, I'm going to see to it that you never work for Vainmill again."

He broke the connection, and wasn't surprised when Oglevie initiated contact with him again a minute later.

"Yeah?" he snapped. "What now?"

"Upon careful reflection, I have decided to deactivate the tramway," replied Oglevie.

Crane allowed himself the luxury of a small smile.

"Good. I'm glad *someone* around here is showing a little sense."

"However, I have appended to the record that I am doing so under protest, and only because my understanding of the current situation is that I am still under your direct command."

"Have you shut it down yet?" asked Crane.

"I'm just about to."

"Then do it."

Crane broke the connection.

"Cupid?"

YES.

"Is there any way to get in or out of the Black Pearl's apartment except by going through her office?"

NO.

"Is there a stairwell in that section of the *Comet*?"

YES.

"Can you lock the door to it on my authority?"

YES.

"If you do, can the Black Pearl order you to open it?"

YES.

"Is there any way I can override her order?"

NO.

Crane frowned and fell silent for a moment. "All right," he said at last. "If you lock it, is there some way I can damage the lock so that it won't open?"

THAT INFORMATION IS CLASSIFIED.

"Thanks," he said. "That's all I needed to know. Let me see a floorplan of the area around the Black Pearl's office."

The diagram appeared.

"Highlight the stairwell," ordered Crane. He studied the drawing. "Got it. All right—is Bello still in the apartment?"

YES.

"I'm going over there now. It should take me about five minutes. I want you to sound an alarm siren throughout the Resort if he leaves the apartment."

UNDERSTOOD.

"Then, as soon as the Dragon Lady is through going over the Priority File, tell her to meet me in that bar you have to pass on the way to the Black Pearl's office."

YOU PASS FOUR OF THEM.

"The one that's out in the open, without any walls."

THE XANADU.

"Right. That's the one."

Crane walked to his closet, waited until the door dilated, withdrew a suitcase, and pulled out a laser weapon. Then, tucking it into a shoulder holster, he donned a roomy tunic that didn't show the bulge and walked out the door.

He checked with the computer when he reached the reception foyer, determined that Bello hadn't tried to leave, and within another three minutes he had reached the stairwell. He tested the door, ascertained that Cupid had indeed locked it, withdrew the laser weapon, and trained it on the tiny computer that controlled the lock. He kept it on until the metal around the computer started melting, then holstered it and commanded the door to open.

It didn't budge.

Then he walked to the Xanadu, sat down at a small table in a corner, ordered a glass of fruit juice, and waited. The Dragon Lady appeared some thirty minutes later.

"I'd have been here sooner," she said, seating herself opposite him, "but the tramway isn't working." She paused. "I gather from Paxton that *you're* responsible for that."

"Pull your chair around," said Crane. "You're blocking the view."

She stood up, placed her chair next to his, and sat down again.

"Did you finish viewing the file?" he asked her.

She nodded. "Yes, I did."

"We've got him," said Crane. "Now it's just a matter of waiting him out or going in after him." He turned to her. "I just made sure that he can't get into the stairwell. If he tries to get out, he's got to walk right past us."

"Then why stop the tramway?"

"I did it initially to make sure he didn't use it before I got here from my suite. But now I think we'd better leave the power off; after all, we can't stay here forever. Sooner or later circumstances are going to be such that he's closer to the tram entrance than we are. At least this way he'll have to be in plain sight for more than a mile in the Mall."

"I see." She stared into Crane's eyes. "Then you definitely want him?"

"Of course I do. Don't you?"

She shook her head. "No," she said seriously. "No, I don't."

"Look—word is going to get out that he was here no matter how we try to hush it up. I gave you credit for being a little smarter than the Black Pearl."

"I know that."

"Then what's your problem?"

"Has it occurred to you that Bello might have been telling the truth?"

"Not really."

"I had the computer try to check his story out," said the Dragon Lady. "Most of it is classified, but there are just enough tidbits of information laying around to convince me that he ordered the air strike for the reason he gave."

"So what?" said Crane. "That doesn't change anything."

"I think it does," she said adamantly. "You know what they'll do to him if we turn him in."

"That's not our concern. Our job is to apprehend him."

"Our job is to apprehend the murderer of Edward Infante."

"Our job is to provide for the security of the *Velvet Comet*," replied Crane. "That security is in danger as long as an escaped mass murderer is aboard."

"You don't believe that for a minute," said the Dragon Lady.

"What the hell do *you* think we should do?" demanded Crane. "Let him stay?"

"Let him walk."

"The biggest fish in the Republic just grabbed our bait, and you want to turn him loose?" he said unbelievingly.

"That's right."

"You're crazy!"

"Perhaps. But that's what I think we should do."

"And what about Pagliacci? You think *he* won't blow the whistle?"

"He doesn't even know Bello has arrived. Arrest Pagliacci now and he'll never know."

Crane stared at her for a long moment, then shook his head.

"I can't do it. I've waited too long for a break like this."

"Even if he's innocent?"

"Innocent of what? He killed 11,000 people."

"Based on inaccurate information."

"Do you know that for a fact?" demanded Crane.

"No," admitted the Dragon Lady.

"Do you know for a fact that he ordered the air strike?"

"Yes."

"Then the only thing you *know* is that he's responsible for 11,000 deaths. You're only guessing about *why* he did it."

"I can make a couple of other guesses, too, if you're willing to listen to them," she said.

"Go ahead."

"My first guess is that the government is going to be very unhappy with you if you arrest him."

"Why?"

"Because this is Deluros, not some little backwater colony world like New Sumatra. They'll never be able to keep the trial secret once the press learns he's been captured, and if he's telling the truth he can cause the government considerable embarrassment."

Crane shook his head. "The people he served have been out of office for nine years."

"What he served was the continuing government of the Republic, and once the facts come out the government will be liable for 11,000 punitive damage suits if he's found innocent—and since no administration is going to pay that much money for another administration's error, they'll find some way to discredit what he says and come in with a guilty verdict. It'll just be another kangaroo court."

He stared at her in silence for a moment.

"And your second guess?"

"That the military will like it even less than the government. They're either going to have to admit that they raised a genocidal maniac to a position of authority, or they're going to have to argue that under certain circumstances 11,000 innocent civilian deaths is an acceptable solution to a problem."

"Very good points," he said. "Now let me pose a single question: What do you think will happen to you and me when word gets out that we let him get away without lifting a finger to stop him?"

"I don't know."

"Well, *I* do," said Crane. "If we're lucky enough not to get blown away by some misguided patriot, I think it's not unreasonable to say that we'll never work again, and that we'll be viewed as outcasts and traitors everywhere we go."

"We could give our reasons," said the Dragon Lady.

"I agree—but if we're going to embarrass the government and the military anyway, why not arrest the son of a bitch and get ourselves off the hook?"

"Then the only alternative, as I see it, is to make sure that no one ever knows he was here."

He shook his head. "You can't prevent it. Pagliacci will know as soon as his people contact him—and you can't hold him incommunicado forever. The Black Pearl knows, and there's always a chance she'll let it slip. You and I know. Bello knows—and what's to keep him quiet once he's safe again? Anyone with my security clearance can order Cupid to open the Priority File—and once I'm off the ship, anyone with *your* clearance can do the same. And *that's* just the people who are *on* the *Comet* right now. Somebody brought him up here; somebody's got to take him away. There are too damned many people involved in this."

"I disagree," said the Dragon Lady. "The only people involved are you, me, the Black Pearl, and Pagliacci. If anyone spotted him on the way up, word would be out by now; and we can see to it that no one spots him on the way out. As for the computer, no one will want to access that file unless you give them a reason to—and if you don't tell anyone he was here, they won't have a reason."

"Is that everything you have to say on the subject, or have you got something else?" asked Crane.

"No, I believe that covers it."

"All right," he said decisively. "I've listened to your arguments, and I've concluded that they don't justify letting Quintus Bello leave the ship free as a bird. The man's a convicted killer, an escaped convict, and a hell of a trophy. The only question remaining is whether we lay siege to him or try to roust him out."

"No, Mr. Crane," said the Dragon Lady. "There's another question to be answered as well."

"What?"

"How long can you stay on watch before you fall asleep?" she asked. "Because I won't be a party to this."

"I'm ordering you to."

"My primary duty is to secure the safety of the ship and its patrons," she replied. "In my professional opinion, the only threat to that safety is Pagliacci. He has already murdered one of our patrons, and I don't think he'd hesitate to kill again if he thought it might lead to Bello's apprehension. As for Bello, I don't believe that he represents a threat of any sort whatsoever." She paused. "I don't think obeying your order is in the best interest of the *Comet*."

"So you're on *her* side," he said coldly.

"I suppose I am," said the Dragon Lady. "I think my reasons are more valid than hers, but when all is said and done, both of us are pledged to protect the *Velvet Comet*."

"He's going to be taken with you or without you," said Crane. "You've just made a very poor career decision."

"I can live with it."

"Do you plan to sit on the sidelines, or are you thinking of actively helping Bello escape?"

"I haven't decided yet."

"Then I suggest you consider your next step very carefully," said Crane. "I can be a formidable enemy."

"I don't doubt it," said the Dragon Lady. She paused. "I have the utmost admiration for you, Mr. Crane. You came up here and in something less than three days you solved a murder and lured Quintus Bello out of hiding. That takes an inordinate amount of talent. But now you're letting your ambition get in the way of your common sense, and if I have to choose between you and the *Comet*, I'll take the *Comet* every time."

"You and the Black Pearl keep talking about it as if

it's something more than a brothel," said Crane. "It's a little bigger and brighter than most, but it's just a whorehouse. If you want to talk about something unique, talk about Quintus Bello."

She shook her head vigorously. "Bello's just a man who made a poor decision based on incomplete information, the same decision you or I might have made. But the *Comet* is something special."

Crane snorted derisively.

"It is, Mr. Crane. It's *more* than a brothel."

"So it's got gambling and restaurants. There are lots of resorts; there's only one Bello."

"It's more than a resort," she continued adamantly. "It's a refuge from reality, a place where everyone—patrons and employees alike—can don those masks that you view with such disfavor, and participate in a universe where, for a few fleeting hours, there is no Quintus Bello."

"Well, it's not *my* universe," he said with finality. "Mine is filled with mountains and chasms, and Quintus Bello is my stepladder to the tallest peak there is."

"Regardless of the consequences?"

"You keep talking about it as if he wasn't a convicted mass murderer," said Crane. "Or as if the *Velvet Comet* will go out of business tomorrow if I capture him today. They're both erroneous assumptions."

"We all may wear masks up here," said the Dragon Lady. "But you wear blinders. Nothing is as open-and-shut and clear-cut as you would like to believe, and especially not this case."

"We'll see," he replied. "In the meantime, if you won't help me, I strongly suggest that you don't try to hinder me." He stared coldly at her. "That means, for starters, that I expect the power to stay off in the tramway."

"I'll give you fair warning before I turn it back on," she said.

"One other thing," said Crane. "Pagliacci is the one who wants him alive. I just want him, period."

"What does that mean?"

"It means don't stand too close to him if we start shooting."

"Nothing will make you change your mind?" she asked, getting to her feet.

"The Black Pearl tried to buy me off, but she overvalued what she had to sell," said Crane. "What's *your* offer?"

"I haven't one."

"Good. That saves me the trouble of refusing it."

She looked down at him and sighed. "You have the capacity to be a truly remarkable man," she said at last. "I hope that if you are confronted with a similar situation 15 years from now you're not still so hungry that you make the wrong decision again."

"We'll just have to wait and see, won't we?" said Crane.

"Let's hope we're all still alive then," she said, turning on her heel and walking away.

13.

Crane sat up abruptly when he heard the pounding on the door.

"Cupid, who is it?"

PAGLIACCI.

"Let him in."

He got off the bed and walked to the living room just as the comedian was stepping through the doorway.

"Hi, Andy," said Pagliacci, shooting him a big smile and heading off toward the bar. "I hope I didn't wake you up."

"I was just dozing," said Crane, smoothing his hair back with his hands.

"Mind if I ask you a question?"

"Go ahead."

"Where is he?"

"Where is *who?*" responded Crane.

Pagliacci chuckled as he poured himself a drink.

"Come on, Andy," he said easily. "I already told you that it makes me nervous when you pretend to be stupid."

"You're talking about Bello?" asked Crane. "How the hell should *I* know? Still on Deluros, I suppose."

"I'm going to ask you politely one more time," said Pagliacci. "Where is he?"

"You think he's on the *Comet*?"

"Oh, no," said Pagliacci with a grin. "I *know* he's on the *Comet*. What I don't know is why you're lying to me."

"What makes you so sure that I'm lying?"

"I'm not blind, Andy. Neither you nor the Dragon Lady are standing watch, and the tramway has been shut down. He's somewhere in the Resort, all right, and you've seen to it that he's going to stay here. Why? Are you negotiating some kind of buy-off?"

"No."

"Then what's going on?"

Crane sighed and sat down on his contour chair. "You're going to find out anyway," he said at last. "I might as well lay it out for you."

"I think that would be your best bet," agreed Pagliacci.

"He got by us during the Dragon Lady's watch."

"How?"

"Disguised himself as a cargo hand and went right to the service level below the tramway," replied Crane. "Evidently Morales was to make contact instantly, and he knew right away that he'd walked into a trap." Crane grimaced. "So he went directly to the Black Pearl's office."

"And claimed sanctuary?"

Crane shook his head. "He didn't have to claim a damned thing. All he did was tell her who he was, and she decided that she didn't want any kind of a scene aboard her ship."

"Too bad for her," said Pagliacci, downing his drink and pouring himself another. "She's got it whether she wants it or not."

"It's not that simple," said Crane.

"Oh? Why not?"

"Because the Dragon Lady is on her side."

"That's some partner you picked for us, Andy," said Pagliacci, frowning. "Steadfast, loyal, and true."

"She has her reasons."

"What possible reason could she have for defending that madman?" asked Pagliacci contemptuously.

"She heard his version of what happened."

"I'll bet it was a dandy," said Pagliacci. "Did he try to throw his body in the path of the planes when they were taking off?"

"No. It was more rational than that."

Pagliacci snorted derisively.

"It was," repeated Crane. He paused. "*I* believe him, too."

"What the hell did he say?" demanded Pagliacci.

"That radio contact with the medical ship was lost, and the Republic dispatched a second ship on the assumption the first one had been disabled, and that he ordered the air strike because the second ship couldn't arrive in time to save the people in the hospital camps, and this was the only way to stop the disease from spreading."

"Bullshit!" yelled Pagliacci.

"You were there," said Crane. "*Was* there a second ship?"

"How the hell do I know?" snapped Pagliacci. "I was too busy burying what was left of my family!"

"It would have arrived about ten or twelve days after the air strike."

"I don't remember any ship!" said Pagliacci. "All I remember are two fucking craters in the ground where 11,000 people had been!"

"Well, that's his story."

"It's a goddamned lie!"

Crane shrugged. "Perhaps."

"And now you're on his side?" continued Pagliacci.

"No."

"Good for you, Andy," said the comedian. "You just increased your life expectancy."

Crane stared at him and said nothing.

"He's still in the madam's office?" asked Pagliacci.

"Yes. I haven't decided whether to go in after him or wait him out."

"Who's watching him?"

"The computer. It'll tell me if he tries to leave."

"Where's the Dragon Lady?"

"Back at Security headquarters, last time I checked," said Crane.

"Then there's nobody in the Black Pearl's office except her and Bello," said Pagliacci. "Let's go in and grab him."

"It's not that easy."

"Why the hell not?"

"Because right now the Dragon Lady is neutral. The second we make a move, she could order Security to oppose us."

"You outrank her. Tell the guards to obey you."

"Their first job is to protect the ship," said Crane patiently. "If we try to break into the madam's office, there's only one response they'll be able to make—or do you plan to kill every Security guard on the ship, too?"

"If I have to."

"Don't be an ass," said Crane. "The way the situation is shaping up, force is our last resort."

Pagliacci scrutinized his face for a moment, then shrugged. "All right. How do *you* suggest we go about getting our hands on him?"

"I'm not sure yet, but I'm leaning toward offering him a deal."

"What kind of deal?"

"Safe passage to Deluros and an open trial."

"He'll never buy it," said Pagliacci firmly. "He's guilty as sin."

"Still, it can't hurt to offer it," said Crane. He turned to the screen. "Cupid!"

YES?

"Patch me through to the Black Pearl's office."

WORKING . . .

The Black Pearl's image appeared a moment later.

"What do you want?" she said coldly.

"Let me talk to Bello."

"No."

"I've got a proposal for him."

"So what?"

"Don't you think he ought to at least be allowed to listen to it?"

She stared at his image for a moment.

"I'll see if he's interested in talking to you," she said, walking out of the range of the camera.

Crane turned to Pagliacci. "*You* keep your mouth shut while I'm talking."

The comedian made no reply, and didn't even acknowledge that he'd heard the statement.

"I'm warning you . . ." continued Crane. Then Bello's image was in front of him, and he turned to face it. "Mr. Bello."

"Mr. Crane."

"I've got a deal to offer you."

"Who is that person next to you?" asked Bello.

"Never mind," said Crane.

"Is he the one who killed Infante?"

"Yes," said Pagliacci.

"Edward Infante was a good and decent man," said Bello grimly, staring at Pagliacci's image. "You have much to answer for, sir."

"Why, you fucking hypocrite!" bellowed Pagliacci. "With all the blood you've got on your hands, you have the gall to—"

"*Shut up!*" yelled Crane, and Pagliacci, momentarily startled, fell silent. "Are you interested in hearing my proposition or not, Mr. Bello?"

"Go ahead," said Bello, still glaring at Pagliacci.

"If I can promise you safe passage to Deluros and a public trial by the military, will you surrender yourself into my custody?"

"No."

"I thought all you wanted was your day in court," persisted Crane.

"By a jury of my peers," answered Bello. "You have the Secretary of the Republic promise me, in writing, that I will be judged by a panel of military governors, and I will place myself under your protective custody."

"There's never been a jury composed solely of military governors," said Crane.

"Then I won't be able to get a fair trial on Deluros, and I will not agree to your terms."

"Then name your planet."

"Not interested, Mr. Crane."

"You don't want a trial at all, do you?" said Crane.

"I see no point in extending our conversation, Mr. Crane," replied Bello, reaching his hand out and breaking the connection.

There was a momentary silence, which Pagliacci finally broke.

"I told you he'd never buy it. *Now* are you ready to go over there and drag him out?"

"Not yet."

"Well," said the comedian, walking around the bar and heading back to the doorway, "I'll give you a little more time to work things out peaceably, Andy. I've been patient for ten years; another few hours won't hurt."

"Thanks for small favors," said Crane sardonically.

"It's a *big* favor," replied Pagliacci. "There's something else you should know."

"Oh?"

The comedian nodded. "Ten years is just about my limit."

"I can't say that I'm flabbergasted."

"I'm not joking, Andy," said Pagliacci. "I'm giving you until midnight to extricate him peacefully."

"And then?" asked Crane dryly.

"And then we do it *my* way—and God help anyone who stands between me and Quintus Bello."

14.

The Black Pearl carried the two trays to her dining room, placed them on the polished table, and ordered Cupid to activate her apartment's intercom system.

"Dinner's ready, Mr. Bello," she announced.

He entered the room a moment later.

"It looks exquisite," he said, looking at the beautifully garnished plates.

"It is," she replied, sitting down at the head of the table and gesturing for him to sit opposite her. "We have the finest chefs in the Republic working for us."

"You didn't make it yourself?" he asked, obviously disturbed.

"Do I look like a cook?"

"Then it was sent here from the kitchen."

"From one of them."

"Does Crane have access to the various kitchens?"

"Of course."

Bello stared at the plate for a moment, then pushed it to the center of the table.

"It's not poisoned, Mr. Bello," the Black Pearl assured him.

"A man in my position can't afford to take chances."

"Can a man in your position afford to starve to death?" she asked.

"I'm not hungry," he said with finality.

"Maybe I can change your mind," she said. "Cupid?"

YES?

"Have either Mr. Crane or Pagliacci visited any of our kitchens, or been in contact with the waiter who just delivered this food?"

NO.

The Black Pearl smiled at Bello. "See? All that worry for nothing. Now enjoy your meal."

"No, thank you. Someone in the kitchen may have found out that I'm here and acted on his own."

The Black Pearl sighed. "I don't know how to tell you this gently, Mr. Bello, but you're yesterday's news."

"I don't understand what you mean."

"Pagliacci's got a personal grudge against you, and Mr. Crane sees you as a means of advancing his career, and of course our patrons are, by and large, very well-informed—but most of the employees aboard the *Comet* probably don't even know who you are or what you've done."

"Rubbish!"

"Truth," she responded. "New Sumatra's a long, long way from here, both in space and in time. There have been a lot of notorious people in the headlines since you dropped out of sight—and your name really doesn't belong up there in lights with, say, Adolph Hitler and Conrad Bland. In fact, if Mr.

Crane was a little higher up in the Vainmill organization, I don't think he'd bother with you at all, given the problems that arresting you will entail. I don't want to hurt your feelings, but you're really a rather minor villain."

"How comforting," he said dryly.

"Well, at least it means you don't have to starve to death."

She began eating her dinner. He watched her very carefully for a few moments, then shrugged, reached for his plate, and took a tentative mouthful.

"Well?" she asked.

"It's very good," he admitted.

"Poisoned?"

"I hope not," he replied, taking another bite.

"I'd offer to ease your mind by trading plates with you," she said, "but since nobody had any way of knowing which of us would be eating from which plate, it seems rather pointless."

"I agree," said Bello, digging into his meal with a vengeance.

"May I offer you some wine?" she asked, opening a bottle and filling her own glass.

"No, thanks," he replied. "I'll keep my risks to a minimum."

"Well, now I know how you've managed to live so long," she said with a shrug.

"It hasn't been easy. I've been in constant danger ever since I escaped from prison."

"Why did you choose to hide out on Deluros?"

He smiled. "It was not unlike the deserter hiding out in the middle of a battlefield. For all practical purposes Deluros VIII is the capital world of the Republic; it's only a matter of time before it officially supersedes Earth. It struck me that this was the last place they'd think of looking for me."

"That seems logical," she admitted.

"It worked for about eight years," he continued. "But they've been closing in on me recently, and it became imperative that I leave."

"They? You mean the government?"

"I assume so—though their methods have been so brutal that it may well be some organization of New Sumatran vigilantes bent on revenge. I really couldn't say." He looked across the table at her. "I'm just thankful that you believe in me."

"I don't," said the Black Pearl.

"I beg your pardon?"

"I believe that people are ultimately responsible for their actions. An awful lot of people died because you made a wrong decision. I think you belong in jail."

"But you heard my explanation!"

"I think it was inadequate."

"In what way?" he demanded.

"You ordered the air strike on your own authority," she answered. "Nobody told you to do it. If the disease hadn't spread in twelve days, it probably wouldn't have spread if you'd have waited two more days until the ship was due. You may have had bad information, but you're the one who acted on it—not the Republic, not your advisors, not your underlings. You killed 11,000 people, Mr. Bello, and all the explanations in the world won't change that."

"Then why didn't you turn me over to Crane?"

"As I said, people are responsible for their actions, and my primary responsibility is the well-being of the *Velvet Comet*. I've been entrusted with its care and protection, and you simply aren't important enough to betray that trust."

"Are you saying that you consider a whorehouse to be more important than me?" he demanded.

"Precisely."

"I suppose I should be grateful," he said coldly, "but that's the most ridiculous statement I've ever heard."

"Then settle for being grateful," replied the Black Pearl.

"I made the most important decision of my life after assessing which actions would serve the greatest number of human beings. You've made yours by judging the fate of a man against a whorehouse!"

"Don't flatter yourself. This was really a very small, simple decision."

"I don't know what's become of our values when a whorehouse is considered more important than a man."

"The *Comet's* not just *any* whorehouse," she said, "and you're not just *any* man."

"A whorehouse is a whorehouse!" he snapped. "It's symptomatic of the lack of character of our government that it's allowed to exist at all!"

"Do you oppose all things erotic, or merely those that cost money?"

"No matter what *you* think, I am a moral man," said Bello. "And I believe that uncontrolled passions cloud men's judgement."

"Was it passion that clouded your judgement when you were on New Sumatra?" she asked calmly.

"Nothing clouded my judgement!" he yelled. "I did the right thing!" He glared at her. "I suppose it's my own fault for thinking that a whore could understand something like that. It's totally beyond your realm of experience."

"It certainly is," she agreed. "I have never been called upon to kill anyone."

"I served the Republic to the best of my ability," he continued doggedly. "The situation arose and I had to face it."

"Well, I serve Eros to the best of my ability," replied the Black Pearl.

"I hope you're not comparing the two!"

"No, I'm not. Eros is far more important."

"That's just what I'd expect someone like you to say!"

"The job of a madam is to bring pleasure into people's lives. The job of a governor is to bring order. Which do you suppose is more important?"

"Without order there is nothing!"

"Don't be silly," she said. "People have frequently lived without order, and as long as their needs were fulfilled they got by. But try taking their pleasures away and see how long they'll tolerate your order, Mr. Bello."

"To think that I owe my safety to someone who thinks a whorehouse is more important than a man's life!" he muttered.

"May I point out that in this instance I think it's more important than a man's death?" said the Black Pearl with a smile.

"*This* instance?" he repeated.

She nodded. "If I felt that arresting or even killing you was in the best interests of the *Comet*, I wouldn't hesitate to do so."

"Then you admit that there are circumstances under which every person in authority has the right to kill."

"I never denied it," she replied. "I just don't think the circumstances arose on New Sumatra. You jumped the gun."

"All *you've* ever done is jump into bed with anyone who could afford you!" he snapped. "What gives you the right to judge my actions?"

"You've asked for sanctuary aboard my ship," said the Black Pearl. "*That* gives me the right."

"Your ship!" he said contemptuously. "You mean your whorehouse!"

"You keep saying whorehouse as if it's a derogatory word. I assure you that it's not. Vulgar, perhaps, but not derogatory."

"Then it should be."

"What do you know about whorehouses, Mr. Bello?" she said. "Have you ever frequented one?"

"Certainly not."

"If you survive this episode in your life, perhaps you should. You might gain an education."

"I doubt it."

"I don't. The *Velvet Comet* is considerably more than a mere whorehouse, Mr. Bello. We have the finest gourmet chefs, the most elegant casino, the most unique fantasy rooms, the most luxurious decor, the most opulent shopping center, the most complete library of booktapes and cinemas, of any place in the Republic. We cater to both sexes in almost equal quantities. We present our patrons with a total experience, not just a sexual one."

"What are you driving at?"

"Your orderly society requires people to work. *We* are what they're working for."

"The *Velvet Comet* is an exclusive playground for the decadent rich, nothing more," he said resolutely.

"I totally agree, except for the word *decadent*. Since the *Comet* represents an almost unattainable goal, it's only natural that only a relative handful of people *can* obtain what it has to offer. And," she added with finality, "since it is the closest thing to a perfect refuge from the banal and mundane yet created, I won't permit you to be the cause of its destruction."

Bello stared at her across the table, an expression of utter contempt on his stern face. "You are perhaps the most immoral person I have ever encountered," he said.

"That's interesting, coming from the murderer of 11,000 innocent men, women and children."

"It is nevertheless true."

"And when was the last time you looked into a mirror, Mr. Bello?"

"I can live with what I've done."

"Bully for you," said the Black Pearl. "Too bad the same can't be said for your victims."

"You are an evil woman," he continued. "At least Crane and the New Sumatran are acting for what they consider moral reasons."

"Let's be perfectly frank, Mr. Bello," said the Black Pearl. "Do you really care whether I'm serving Eros or Order, as long as I save your ass?"

"I certainly do."

She smiled in amusement. "You're only saying that because you know I'll protect you regardless of what you feel."

"I am speaking the absolute truth."

"Really?"

He glared at her severely. "I don't lie, not even to whores."

"Well," she said, "as long as you don't want the protection of a whore, there might be a way out of this yet. I can't let Mr. Crane and Pagliacci take you back to Deluros, not with the ensuing publicity—but if I offer to turn you over to Pagliacci on the condition that he kills you aboard the *Comet* and promises never to tell what he's done . . ." She let her voice trail off for a moment and watched him shift uncomfortably.

"You can't!" he rasped harshly.

"Oh? Why not?"

"It would be tantamount to murder!"

"Not murder—execution. After all, you're wanted dead or alive."

"You wouldn't know whether you could believe him!" said Bello, starting to fidget in earnest.

"What possible difference can that make to you?" she asked. "If he talked, it would be detrimental to the *Comet*—and you disapprove of the *Comet*."

She watched him squirm for another minute and then laughed aloud.

"Relax, Mr. Bello. I'm not going to give you to Pagliacci. You don't know it, of course, but nothing could keep Mr. Crane quiet. He's not quite the moral paragon you seem to think; in point of fact, he views you as nothing more than a job opportunity. At any rate, you simply aren't worth the trouble he can cause my ship."

"Then why did you say all that?" he demanded.

"I just thought you might like to admit that there are worse things than being under the protection of a whore—such as *not* being under her protection."

"You are a despicable woman!" he snapped, rising to his feet.

"Aren't you staying for dessert?" she asked sweetly.

He left the room without uttering another word.

The Black Pearl finished her meal, cleaned off the table, had the computer check on Crane's and Pagliacci's whereabouts, and spent the next half hour tending to her Night Crystals, all the while wondering why, of the billions upon billions of humans in the galaxy, Quintus Bello had become the one she found herself forced to defend against all enemies.

15.

"Cupid?" said Crane.

YES?

"Put a call through to the Black Pearl."

SHE HAS EXPLICITLY STATED THAT SHE DOES NOT WISH TO RECEIVE ANY COMMUNICATIONS FROM YOU OR PAGLIACCI.

"Do it anyway."

I HAVE BEEN INSTRUCTED NOT TO.

"Tell her it's an emergency."

It took almost a full minute before the Black Pearl's image appeared.

"What is the emergency, Mr. Crane?"

"Where's Lover Boy?" he asked, his eyes scanning the office.

"In the next room."

"Sleeping?"

"Pouting," she answered. "We don't get along very well."

"That's not exactly surprising, considering who he is and what he's done," remarked Crane. "You really ought to turn him over to me."

"Nothing's changed, Mr. Crane. I can't do it."

"Something *has* changed," he corrected her. "It's almost 2100 hours, ship's time."

"I know what time it is," she replied.

"But what you *don't* know is that if you haven't released Bello into my custody by midnight, Pagliacci is coming in after him."

"Alone?"

Crane shook his head. "If I can't stop him, I'll have to join him."

"Why?"

"Because if somebody is going to capture Quintus Bello, it's going to be *me*." He paused. "This thing is getting out of hand. That's why we have to talk."

"We just finished talking Mr. Crane," said the Black Pearl. "And now that you've told me what to expect, I'll have the Dragon Lady order Security to confine Pagliacci to his quarters."

"It's not that simple," said Crane with a grimace. "I don't know where he is."

"I'll ask Cupid."

"Cupid doesn't know either. I've already asked."

She stared at him for a moment, then put the question to the computer and received a negative answer.

"He must be in the tunnel," she concluded.

"I don't know," said Crane dubiously. "He has to figure that's the first place you'd look for him. He's been aboard the ship for a few months; probably he's found half a dozen places to hide where Cupid can't find him."

"Then we'll simply have to ferret him out with search parties."

"I wouldn't do that if I were you," said Crane.

"Why not?"

"Because Infante wasn't the first man he's killed. This guy knows his stuff. Send a Security team after him and I guarantee most of them won't live through the night."

"Then what do you suggest?"

"I don't know," said Crane. "But I think we'd better get together and talk about it sometime in the next half hour."

"You can't come here," she said adamantly. "I don't trust you with Bello in the apartment."

"Then come to my suite."

"Pagliacci might be watching."

"Okay," he said. "You name a place."

"The hunting lodge."

"You mean the fantasy room?"

She nodded. "It's not currently in use, and we won't be overheard."

"Ten minutes?" suggested Crane.

"Make it twenty," she replied. "And I trust you won't mind if I bring the Dragon Lady."

"Be my guest."

He broke the connection, then had Cupid throw a floorplan of the fantasy levels onto the screen and pinpoint the hunting lodge's location. Then, with a few minutes to kill, he had the computer bring up the holograph of the Black Pearl's erotic dance, watched it for the better part of ten minutes, and then began making his way to the appointed meeting place.

He walked down the long corridor, took an elevator to the top level of the Resort, got off, turned to his left, stopped at the fifth door, and ordered it to open.

He stepped through into a splendidly-appointed hunting lodge. The floor was made of some polished hardwood and was covered by half a dozen animal skins, while the walls housed the mounted heads of some twenty animals: there were Baffledivers from Pinnipes II, Devilowls from Alimond, a tiger from Earth itself, even a representation of the supposedly-mythical Dreamwish Beast.

The furniture was all made of tufted leather, the wet bar possessed a matching leather trim, and there was a floor-to-ceiling free-standing stone fireplace in the middle of the room. An oversized wooden bed dominated one corner, and off to one side was a circular whirlpool bath with a cloud of steam rising from the surface.

The back wall of the lodge was composed entirely of interlocking glass doors which led to a sturdy wooden balcony. He slid one of the doors open, and suddenly his ears and nostrils were assailed by an array of strange and exotic sounds and scents. The terrain seemed to extend for miles, the flat grasslands leading to a series of foothills off in the distance. Herds of elephantine herbivores grazed within 50 yards of him, while somewhat farther away he could see a pride of red-tinted catlike carnivores gathered around a kill. He looked up, shading his eyes from the bright yellow sun, and saw a trio of hawklike creatures circling lazily over the carnivores, waiting for their opportunity to swoop down and scavenge the leftovers.

Despite the fact that he knew the fantasy room was no more than 30 by 40 feet, he had to fight the urge to believe utterly in the reality of his surroundings. He could even feel the lodge shake when a group of the herbivores trotted past.

Suddenly he heard the door to the corridor slide open, and he walked back into the lodge. The Black Pearl and the Dragon Lady entered the room and walked over to the grouping of chairs by the roaring but heatless fire.

"This is some room," said Crane, joining them.

"Actually, it's one of our less popular ones," replied the Black Pearl. "Not romantic enough."

"How much of it is real?"

"Everything from the bed to the wet bar. The rest of it comes from about 50 holographic projectors."

He maneuvered an oversized leather chair until it faced both of theirs and then sat down.

"It seems pretty romantic to me," he noted.

"There are too many things to see through the window," answered the Black Pearl. "It tends to take the attention away from where it belongs. However," she added, "we didn't come here to talk about romance."

"No, we didn't," he agreed.

"In fact, we came to talk about a situation that is largely of your own devising," she continued.

"What are you talking about? *I'm* not the one who's planning on breaking into your apartment at midnight."

"But you're the one who lured Quintus Bello here in the first place," said the Black Pearl.

"I think we're getting away from the point," interjected the Dragon Lady. "We have a potentially explosive situation here, and we want to come up with some method of defusing it."

"Simple," said Crane firmly. "Turn Bello over to me and let us leave the *Comet* before midnight."

"That's out of the question," said the Black Pearl.

"It's no longer a case of letting him walk," persisted Crane. "You've really just got two choices: either I take him peacefully, or else Pagliacci takes him forcibly and a bunch of people die in the process. There's no third way."

"There are *always* alternatives," said the Dragon Lady.

"For instance?"

"That's what we're here to discuss," she said. "For example, does Pagliacci plan to enlist your aid at midnight?"

"I suppose so."

"Then he'll make contact with you before he starts to apply force?"

"Probably."

"Well, there's *one* alternative," said the Dragon Lady. "Arrest him when he shows up."

"For how long?" asked Crane. "Sooner or later you've got to release him or turn him over to the authorities, and you can bet that the first two words out of his mouth are going to be 'Quintus Bello'."

"First things first," said the Dragon Lady. "Once we've got him, we'll worry about what to do with him."

"And what do *I* get out of it?"

"I don't understand the question," said the Security Chief. "You will be helping us to make sure no blood is shed."

He shook his head. "Not enough. If I'm going to put my life on the line—and make no mistake about it, that's exactly what you're asking me to do—then I need something more in remuneration than the satisfaction of a job well done."

"You're referring to Bello, of course?" said the Dragon Lady.

"Of course."

"No deal," said the Black Pearl.

"You don't even like him," noted Crane.

"Liking him has nothing to do with it," she replied. "I've explained over and over again: I won't have him apprehended aboard the *Comet*."

"And *I've* explained over and over again that you can't keep this thing quiet," replied Crane in frustration. "If you arrest Bello, he's going to talk; and if you let him go, Pagliacci is going to talk." Suddenly he jumped up. "*Shit*!"

"What's the matter?" asked the Dragon Lady.

"Cupid?" he yelled.

A screen behind the bar flickered to life.

YES?

"Have I been monitored since I arrived here?"

NO.

"Open the Priority File, and make it retroactive to the moment I opened the door to this room."

WORKING . . . DONE.

He turned back to the two women.

"Even if Bello and Pagliacci both turned into saints, gave themselves up, and never said a word about the *Comet*, you'd still have to remember never to mention them again. That's twice I've almost blown it in two days—and *you're* up here full time."

"That is the least of our problems," said the Dragon Lady.

"Right," agreed the Black Pearl. She paused, then

said thoughtfully: "Would Pagliacci be open to a deal?"

"Not the one you offered me," said Crane harshly.

"Don't be crude, Mr. Crane," she replied.

"What kind of deal?"

"What if we agreed to drop the murder charge against him, in exchange for his allowing Bello to leave?"

"Not a chance," said Crane. "He doesn't even think there *is* a murder charge against him."

"We could set him straight on the matter."

"It wouldn't make a bit of difference," said Crane. "You're not dealing with a rational man here."

"He seems rational enough to me."

"Not on the subjct of Bello. He's fighting a holy war, and he's got the religious fervor of a fanatic. Don't forget: he's not just some hit man hired by an impersonal organization. Bello killed his wife and daughters. He's spent more than a decade trying to track him down." Crane paused. "From his point of view, he's showing remarkable restraint by giving me until midnight to get Bello peacefully."

"As I said, he's much more of a threat to the *Comet's* security than Bello," noted the Dragon Lady. "He's killed once, and he's quite willing to kill again. All Bello wants to do is escape."

"I agree," said the Black Pearl. "Pagliacci is our immediate problem, not Bello."

Crane checked his chronometer.

"You've got a little over two hours to solve that particular problem before he goes into action."

"What can he do, really?" asked the Dragon Lady. "I can put 20 guards around the Black Pearl's office."

"I don't know exactly what his capabilities are,"

admitted Crane. "But that's a pretty wide corridor, with no place to hide. He can probably mow half of them down before they know what hit them."

"I can post them *inside* the office," suggested the Dragon Lady.

"No!" snapped the Black Pearl. "How can we keep news of Bello's presence a secret if 20 security guards are rubbing shoulders with him?"

"Look," said Crane. "There's no question that you'll be able to stop him. He may be good, but he's not *that* good. I'm just operating on the assumption that none of our careers will benefit from a bloodbath."

"Correct," said the Black Pearl.

"Tell me, Mr. Crane," said the Dragon Lady. "If you were Pagliacci, how would *you* plan to extricate Bello from the Black Pearl's office?"

"I wouldn't."

"That was a serious question, Mr. Crane."

"I'm giving you a serious answer," replied the detective. "You've got to remember that while Pagliacci is willing to sacrifice his own life, he's not willing to kill Bello. He wants him to stand trial, with all the attendant publicity that will ensue. Now, if I were Pagliacci, I'd figure that the likelihood of reaching Bello at all is pretty small, and the likelihood of taking him alive is almost nil. So I'd threaten to break in, just to make you concentrate your efforts there, and then I'd find a very public place where you couldn't grab me immediately, wait until it was packed with patrons, and then tell them that Bello is aboard the ship and that the madam is protecting him. Sooner or later someone would believe me, and the moment that happened, you'd *have* to turn him over, if not to me then to the authorities on Deluros VIII."

The Dragon Lady stared unhappily at him.

"You know, it makes sense," she said grimly.

"I reluctantly agree," said the Black Pearl. She turned to Crane. "Is he capable of thinking that clearly?"

"I don't know," admitted Crane honestly. "He's not stupid—but he *is* fanatical on the subject of Bello, and I don't know how much that colors his judgement."

"Well, those seem to be our two most likely scenarios," said the Dragon Lady with a sigh. "Either he makes Bello's presence a matter of common knowledge to our patrons, or else a number of people—possibly including some patrons—have to die to prevent it."

"There's a third scenario," Crane reminded them. "Turn Bello over to me right now."

The Black Pearl shook her head. "Even if I did that, it wouldn't stop Pagliacci from talking. *He's* the problem, not Bello. He's the one we have to stop."

"That's why I called this little meeting," said Crane. "To warn you that he's got the bit between his teeth."

"That's not enough," said the Black Pearl.

"What more do you expect me to do?" said Crane caustically. "Kill him and let Bello go?"

"There are worse ideas," said the Dragon Lady, walking over to the bar and pouring herself a creme de cacao.

Crane laughed derisively. "*I* haven't heard any."

"Mr. Crane," continued the Dragon Lady, "I think it's about time that you stopped and reassessed your position. Luring Bello up here may have been a good idea in the beginning, but the situation has gotten out of control. The one thing Vainmill has in common with all governments and major corporations is that it abhors scandals—and it is no longer possible for you to arrest him without causing one. Whether he talks or Pagliacci talks, word is going to get out you allowed one the freedom of the ship and enticed the other to come aboard. I submit to you that this is not really the way to advance your career or your reputation. They pay you to *control* damage, not cause it. I think capturing Bello aboard the *Comet* will make them very unhappy with you."

He stared at her thoughtfully, but made no reply.

"She's right, you know," said the Black Pearl. "You were sent up here to solve a relatively simple problem, and instead you've managed to create a truly complex one. You probably couldn't have foreseen the consequences when you started on this course of action, but now that they're in clearer focus, you'll bear the brunt of the blame if you refuse to help resolve the problem."

He was silent a moment longer, stroking his chin with his right forefinger.

"I can't just let him walk," he said at last. "I mean, hell, he's Quintus Bello!"

"As I find myself pointing out with monotonous regularity, Pagliacci is our immediate problem, not Bello," said the Black Pearl.

"All right," said Crane warily. "Let's say that I go along with you. Suppose I—ah—*neutralize* Pagliacci," he continued, aware that his words were going into Cupid's Priority File. "What then?"

"Then we've bought ourselves some breathing room," replied the Black Pearl.

"Don't play dumb with me!" he snapped. "You know exactly what I mean."

"You still can't arrest him aboard the ship."

"I know," said Crane. "The Dragon Lady has just convinced me of that. But what about *off* the ship?"

"It's an interesting notion," said the Black Pearl. "How would you arrange it?"

"Link Cupid to his escape ship's computer so I can pinpoint where he lands."

"I think I can live with that," said the Black Pearl.

"How about you?" Crane asked the Dragon Lady.

"I have my doubts." She poured herself another glass of liqueur and returned to her chair with it.

"A kangaroo court is a lot better than having Pagliacci kill him," Crane pointed out.

"It's not that," she replied. "I will certainly sacrifice Mr. Bello's right to a fair trial in exchange for the *Comet's* security."

"Then what's the problem?"

"What's to stop him from talking?" asked the Dragon Lady.

"Let him talk from now til doomsday," replied Crane. "Passing through the *Comet* on his escape route is a hell of a lot different from being captured there while the madam is defending him. Besides, he'll have no reason to go into it in detail; he's got quite enough enemies so that I won't have to take the stand against him."

"Well," said the Dragon Lady with a shrug, "it looks like the best deal we can make."

"I know," he agreed glumly. "I was a lot happier when I didn't think I had to make it."

"You've got about two hours in which to solve our problem," noted the Black Pearl.

"I'm aware of that," replied Crane, getting to his feet.

"Have you any idea how you plan to go about it?"

"If I do, my mother didn't raise any children stupid enough to tell you about it while Cupid is capturing this whole conversation for posterity."

"How will we know that the situation has been alleviated?"

Crane walked to the door.

"You'll know," he promised.

16.

"Cupid?"

YES?

"Patch me in to the ship's intercom system."

WORKING . . . DONE.

"All right. I want to send a message to every section of the ship, except those rooms where people are actively copulating at this moment. How do I go about it?"

TELL ME WHEN YOU'RE READY TO BEGIN AND I WILL ACTIVATE THE INTERCOM SPEAKERS.

"Now."

READY.

Crane cleared his throat.

"Ladies and gentlemen," he began. "The *Velvet Comet* invites you to come, as our guests, to Pagliacci's final nightclub performance at 0030 hours this morning. That's half an hour after midnight. Let's give our favorite comedian a rousing sendoff."

IS THAT ALL?

"Yes."

DEACTIVATING INTERCOM . . . DONE.

"Thanks," said Crane. "Now open my door."

The door to his suite slid into the wall, and, when he made no effort to walk out into the corridor, slid shut again.

"No. Leave it open."

The door slid open.

"Okay. You might as well show me the sports headlines while I'm waiting."

Crane sat down in his contour chair, hands clasped behind his head, and spent the next half hour catching up on the latest scores, as an occasional prostitute or patron stopped to look into his suite while walking down the corridor.

Finally one figure stopped in the doorway and didn't move on.

"Hi, Andy. What's all this bullshit about a final performance?"

"Come on in," said Crane, turning to face him.

As the comedian entered the living room, Crane ordered the door to close.

"So what's up?" asked Pagliacci.

"I didn't know how else to reach you," replied Crane. "I had to get a message to you that you don't have to go to war at midnight; this seemed to be the easiest way."

"What kind of deal have you cut?"

"They'll turn Bello over to us tomorrow morning at 0800 hours."

"That was awfully easy," said Pagliacci warily. "What did you have to promise them?"

"That's *my* business," said Crane. "The only thing that should concern you is that we've got him."

"I hope so," said Pagliacci. "Because if I find out you're lying to me, I could become very upset with you." He paused. "You wouldn't like me when I'm upset."

"I've seen you when you're telling jokes," remarked Crane dryly. "How much worse can you get?"

Pagliacci threw back his head and laughed. "I *knew* we were going to get along the first time I met you, Andy!" His laughter ended as quickly as it had begun. "Where do we pick him up?"

"The airlock."

"I don't like it," said the comedian. "Too easy for him to make a break for it. Fix it for us to get him at the Black Pearl's office."

"I'll do what I can," said Crane.

"When and where should you and I meet?"

"How about 0630 hours in the reception foyer?" suggested the detective.

"Sounds good to me," agreed Pagliacci. He walked to the door. "Well, I gotta run. You seem to have obligated me to a final performance."

"You could always skip it," said Crane with feigned nonchalance.

Pagliacci shook his head. "No sense doing anything that might attract attention. Why don't you come by and catch the show? Maybe I'll finally find a way to make you laugh."

"Maybe I will," said Crane, as Pagliacci walked out into the corridor.

Crane gave Pagliacci half an hour to get firmly ensconced in his dressing room, then made his way to the nightclub. He went immediately to the backstage area, scrounged through the prop room until he found what he was after, and shortly thereafter locked himself inside an empty dressing room. Once there, he pulled his pistol out of his pocket, placed it on a table next to the prop, removed a silencer from another pocket, and went to work.

When he was finished, he walked over to the vanity and began carefully applying white grease-paint to his face. It took about fifteen minutes, after which he used some bright red lipstick on his lips and black grease pencil around his eyes. Finally he scrutinized his face in the mirror for a moment and then, satisfied, he leaned back on his chair and relaxed.

The show started half an hour later, and once the house lights dimmed, Crane walked back out into the audience. He checked the room, saw the Black Pearl and the Dragon Lady seated at a table toward the back, and quickly walked over to join them.

"Mr. Crane?" asked the Dragon Lady, after staring at him for a minute.

"Good evening, ladies," he said. "I trust you told the stage manager that Pagliacci will be making an appearance."

"You told me to, didn't you?" said the Black Pearl. "By the way, what's with the make-up? Surely you're not going to impersonate him."

"I'm not that untalented," he replied with a smile.

"All of this *does* have something to do with our little arrangement, doesn't it?" demanded the madam.

"Something," he agreed. "I hope you're going to be a good audience and laugh on cue."

"I don't understand."

"You will," he said. "Just remember to laugh."

He turned and faced the stage as Pagliacci stepped out from behind the curtains. The comedian launched into a discourse about his misadventures in the stock market, segued into his private detective routine, and was soon hard at work building a series of sexual puns that drew groans and laughter in equal proportions. Finally he wound up talking about his visit to a psychiatrist.

"So," he said, "my shrink looks at my charts, and says, 'Based on my examination, I have come to the conclusion that you're crazy.' Well, this kind of pisses me off, so I tell him that I want a second opinion. 'Okay,' he says; 'you're ugly, too.' "

"That's terrible!" shouted Crane above the audience noise.

Pagliacci peered into the darkened room, but was unable to spot the source of the heckling.

He told another joke, and Crane got to his feet.

"Come on, Pagliacci!" he yelled. "The last time I saw a face like yours it had a fish hook in its mouth."

A couple of nearby patrons tried to shush him, then noticed his make-up and assumed that he must be a part of the act.

Pagliacci finally pinpointed the area the heckling was coming from.

"Ladies and gentlemen," he said, pointing in Crane's direction, "let me present a mathematical paradox: three heels in one pair of shoes."

Suddenly Crane raced to the stage and clambered up onto it.

"Who the hell are you?" demanded the comedian.

Crane ignored him and pulled out his pistol.

"I can't stand it anymore!" he screamed, mugging at the audience. "If I hear one more bad joke, I'll go crazy!"

He touched a button on the weapon's handle, and

a small banner with the word *BANG* emblazoned on it flew down from the barrel.

Suddenly the Black Pearl and the Dragon Lady shrieked with laughter, and a moment later the whole audience followed suit. As the laughter built to a crescendo, Crane pulled the trigger on his weapon.

Pagliacci's hands flew up over his head and he spun around, a look of total astonishment on his face. He tried to say something, but couldn't seem to get the words out. Crane leaped across the stage, caught him just before he fell into the audience, and slung him over one shoulder. The crowd applauded with delight.

"Pagliacci thanks you for your response, and invites you to see his all-new act, starting next month on Lodin XI," he announced, bowing as low as he could without dropping the body, then parting the curtains and walking backstage before the blood from the tiny hole in the comedian's chest had spread enough to become visible.

He carried the corpse to his dressing room, activated his Priority File, laid the body on a table, and began washing off his make-up. The door opened a moment later, and he could hear the voice of the headlining singer for an instant as the Black Pearl and the Dragon Lady stepped through.

"Is he dead?" asked the Black Pearl.

"Of course he's dead," replied Crane.

"Nice and neat."

"Not so neat," he said irritably, displaying his blood-spattered tunic. "The son of a bitch ruined my outfit."

"I'm sure you can afford a new one," remarked the Black Pearl dryly.

"In the meantime," said the Dragon Lady, "the audience is still talking about what a unique exit Pagliacci made." She shook her head in amazement. "You'd think *somebody* out there would know that they had just witnessed a murder!"

"Why?" said Crane. "The nightclub's just like the rest of the *Comet*."

"I don't think I follow you."

"They come here to watch people in masks act out a bunch of fantasies. Why should shooting Pagliacci be any more real than anything else that happens up here?"

"That's why you chose to eliminate him in the nightclub?" asked the Black Pearl.

He nodded. "Any place with a crowd would have done as well. The more people who saw it, the less chance there was that anyone would believe it. It just happened to be easier to lure him to the club than anywhere else." He paused. "I could have shot him in my suite, I suppose, but it would be a hell of a lot harder to explain. I'd have had to hide it in the Priority File, and sooner or later someone would open it up and you'd have a whole new can of worms to deal with. This way we've got 300 witnesses who will swear he was smiling and waving to them the last time they saw him, and I'll swear to Vainmill that I arrested him and had to shoot him when he attempted to escape."

"I still can't believe we got through it that easily," said the Black Pearl. She sighed. "All we have to do now is get Bello off the ship and we're done."

"What will you do with the body?" asked the Dragon Lady.

"I'll be taking it back to Deluros with me," he

replied. "After all, I was sent up here to solve a murder. *He's* my solution."

"I can have some of my Security people move him to your ship," she offered.

"Thanks. And make sure he isn't recognized."

"We're not in the habit of carrying corpses through the Resort. He'll be placed in some kind of container."

Crane turned to the Black Pearl.

"When are you letting Bello go?"

"As soon as I get back to my office."

"Before you do, get me the registration number on his ship. I've got to give it to Cupid so he can keep tabs on it."

"All right. Will you be here for another half hour?"

"I don't know. How long before we can move the body?"

"I can stay here with it until my people come," said the Dragon Lady.

"Can they be trusted?" asked Crane.

"Probably," she replied. "But just to be on the safe side, I'll remove his make-up before they get here." She smiled. "They'll never know who they're moving."

"Good," said Crane. "In that case, I'm going to go back to my suite and relax. It's been a long day."

"Do you want the information on the ship sent there, then?" asked the Black Pearl.

"Right," he said. "And while you're at it, send along a companion. I think I owe myself a little celebration."

"Did you have anyone in mind?"

He stared at her for a long moment, then sighed.

"Bo Peep," he said at last. "Without her sheep, if possible," he added wryly.

"You're sure you wouldn't prefer someone else?" she asked meaningfully.

"I'm sure." He smiled. "Why spoil a beautiful enmity just for a roll in the hay?"

She shrugged and left the room as he went back to removing his make-up.

17.

Crane waited until the Black Pearl's door slid open, then stepped into her office, where the madam and the Dragon Lady were waiting for him.

"Good morning, Mr. Crane," said the Black Pearl. "I trust you—ah—slept well?"

"After a fashion," he replied. "I just thought I'd stop by to go over some final details before I head back to Deluros."

"Have a seat," said the Black Pearl. "Can I get you some coffee?"

Crane nodded. "I could do with a cup."

He walked over to a sofa, sat down on it, and turned to the Dragon Lady.

"Is my cargo loaded?"

"Both of them," she replied.

"Both?"

"Pagliacci and Infante."

"I'd forgotten all about Infante," he admitted. "I suppose he's State's Exhibit Number One."

"I was wondering what you want to do about Morales?" asked the Security Chief.

"Wait until I'm off the ship and turn him loose," answered Crane.

She frowned. "Just like that?"

"What can he do—go to the authorities and say we tricked him into betraying Quintus Bello? He's got a lot more to hide than we do." He paused. "While you're at it, you might tell him we nailed Infante's killer."

The Black Pearl returned with a cup of black coffee, which she handed to him.

"Thank you," said Crane. "By the way, what time did Bello take off?"

"About five hours ago," replied the Black Pearl. "How soon will you be going after him?"

Crane shrugged noncommittally. "I've got a lot of other things to do first. Besides, Cupid can tell me where to find him if I want him."

"*If* you want him?" repeated the Black Pearl. "I thought that was what this whole situation was about."

"I've got to sound out Vainmill first," explained Crane. He turned back to the Dragon Lady. "I have a feeling you might be right: bringing in Bello could be bad for business all the way around."

"Speaking of Vainmill," interjected the Black Pearl, "will they give you any trouble about coming back with *two* corpses?"

"As long as nobody figures out what was going on up here, I should be all right," he said.

"And if somebody *does* figure it out?" she persisted.

"He'll be all right anyway," broke in the Dragon Lady.

"I hope you're right," said Crane.

"I know I am," she replied. "Do you think this is the first scandal the *Comet* has ever had to hush up?

We've had more crimes and criminals up here than you can imagine, Mr. Crane. We've caught heads of state cheating in the casino, we've had high governmental officials go a little haywire while practicing some of the more exotic sexual disciplines, we've even had a madam murdered. All Vainmill has ever asked is that we contain the damage and hush up the scandal—and when they finally figure out that we had Quintus Bello aboard the *Comet*, they'll know that you took the proper course of action." She paused. "When someone actually gets around to opening that Priority File during one of Cupid's regular audits—as sooner or later someone will—you just may come out of this in even better shape than you thought."

He finished his coffee and got to his feet.

"Well, I guess I'd better be going," he announced.

"We'll miss you, Mr. Crane," said the Dragon Lady, rising and shaking his hand.

"Some of you less than others," he replied with a glance at the Black Pearl.

"Perhaps," acknowledged the Dragon Lady. "Just the same, I'd take an early retirement if there were any way I could induce you to become the *Comet's* Security Chief."

He uttered an amused chuckle. "I'm supposed to be going *up* Vainmill's ladder, not *down* it."

"Stated with your customary sensitivity," commented the Black Pearl.

He walked to the door, then turned to the madam. "Can I ask you a question?" he said.

"Go ahead."

"I've got two corpses aboard my ship, you've just turned a mass murderer loose, and somewhere in the guts of that computer is a file that could conceivably send us all to the gallows."

"What is your question, Mr. Crane?"

"Do you think it was worth it?"

She smiled. "Pagliacci is dead, Bello is in hiding, Morales will never tell what little he knows, and you're leaving for Deluros VIII. The only thing that remains intact is the *Velvet Comet*." She paused. "What do *you* think?"

"I think it's a pretty high price to pay for a little sex," he remarked dryly.

"You're entitled to your opinion," she replied.

He waited to see if she had any further comment, then shrugged and left the office.

"A most unusual man," said the Dragon Lady, when the door had slid shut again.

"I didn't like him," replied the Black Pearl.

"I know. He was an unusual man anyway. I'll miss him."

"You'll have a dessert or two, and get back to work, and miss him a lot less," said the Black Pearl. "Men come and go. Only the *Comet* remains."

"I suppose so," said the Dragon Lady. She kept her gaze on the doorway through which Crane had departed. "I wonder if he'll make it?"

"To Deluros?" asked the madam, puzzled.

"To the chairmanship."

"I doubt it. Too impulsive."

"Still, in the end he did the right thing."

"Only because he had no choice," noted the Black Pearl. "He was a very dangerous man."

"He was a very brilliant man."

"I know. That's what made him so dangerous." She sighed. "Well, I suppose if the *Velvet Comet* can survive a friend like him, it can survive anything." She stood up. "I'm going to feed my Night Crystals now. Would you care to come along and watch?"

"No," said the Dragon Lady. "I've got to get back to work."

"I'll see you later."

The Dragon Lady nodded and walked out the door, and was back in her own office ten minutes later. She went directly to the built-in refrigerator, took out an incredibly rich chocolate pastry, and sat down at her desk.

"Cupid?"

YES?

"Bring up the outside viewscreen, please. I'd like to see Mr. Crane's ship."

A holograph of the ship appeared instantly.

The funny part, she reflected as she nibbled daintily at the pastry and watched the ship speed away, was that the Black Pearl was right: already the feeling of regret caused by his departure was lessening. She smiled as she tried to imagine his reaction had he known of her attraction to him, then shrugged. When all was said and done he was just a man, as flawed and ephemeral as any other man or woman. There would come a day, and not too far off at that, when she wouldn't even be able to remember what he looked like. The only thing of substance, the only thing that lasted, was the *Comet*.

And, since one of the things it represented was indulgence in one's personal passions, she finished her pastry with only a minimal sense of guilt. Then, sated spiritually as well as physically, she summoned her staff and began going over the day's duty roster.

About the Author

MIKE RESNICK was born in Chicago in 1942, attended the University of Chicago (where, in the process of researching his first adventure novel, he earned three letters on the fencing team and was nationally ranked for a brief period), and married his wife, Carol, in 1961. They have one daughter, Laura.

From the time he was 22, Mike has made his living as a professional writer. He and Carol have also been very active at science fiction conventions, where Mike is a frequent speaker and Carol's stunning costumes have swept numerous awards at masquerade competitions.

Mike and Carol were among the leading breeders and exhibitors of show collies during the 1970s, a hobby which led them to move to Cincinnati and purchase a boarding and grooming kennel.

Mike has received several awards for his short stories and an award for a nonfiction book for teenagers. His first love, though, remains science fiction, and his excellent science fiction novels—THE SOUL EATER, BIRTHRIGHT: THE BOOK OF MAN, WALPURGIS III, SIDESHOW, THE THREE-LEGGED HOOTCH DANGER, THE WILD ALIEN TAMER, THE BEST ROOTIN' TOOTIN' SHOOTIN' GUNSLINGER IN THE WHOLE DAMNED GALAXY, THE BRANCH, and EROS ASCENDING—are also available in Signet editions.